# In Pursuit of Love, Spirituality, and happiness

# In Pursuit of Love, Spirituality, and happiness

*Gita Audhya*

iUniverse, Inc.
New York  Bloomington

# In Pursuit of Love, Spirituality and Happiness

*Copyright © 2009 by Gita Audhya*

*All rights reserved. No part of this book may be used or reproduced by any means, graphic, electronic, or mechanical, including photocopying, recording, taping or by any information storage retrieval system without the written permission of the publisher except in the case of brief quotations embodied in critical articles and reviews.*

*This is a work of fiction. All of the characters, names, incidents, organizations, and dialogue in this novel are either the products of the author's imagination or are used fictitiously.*

*iUniverse books may be ordered through booksellers or by contacting:*

*iUniverse*
*1663 Liberty Drive*
*Bloomington, IN 47403*
*www.iuniverse.com*
*1-800-Authors (1-800-288-4677)*

*Because of the dynamic nature of the Internet, any Web addresses or links contained in this book may have changed since publication and may no longer be valid. The views expressed in this work are solely those of the author and do not necessarily reflect the views of the publisher, and the publisher hereby disclaims any responsibility for them.*

*ISBN: 978-1-4401-3989-5 (pbk)*
*ISBN: 978-1-4401-3990-1 (ebk)*

*Printed in the United States of America*

*iUniverse rev. date: 6/30/2009*

# Chapter 1

Hawaii, eight islands of eternal spring, where the sun, abiding by its assurance to the ancient Hawaiian God Maui who had once lassoed it, travels at its slowest. Hawaii, land of gentle breezes and bright sunshine, home of the graceful hula, the lei, the surfboard, Pele, the Goddess of Volcanic Fire and the protected bay, Honolulu, settled almost a thousand years ago but now home only to the new. Honolulu, ringed by splendid beaches including that world-famous sun-seeker and surfer's paradise, Waikiki. Honolulu of open shirts and sunburned skins, of thong bikinis, flowered shirts, and wild print dresses of ageless beauty.

"The expected time of arrival at Honolulu International Airport is 13.40 hours, just five minutes away. The temperature there is a pleasant 25 degrees Celsius. Please return to your seats and fasten your safety belts." The pilot's resonant voice broke in on his reverie, and Jonathan reset his very expensive Rolex watch, a present from his mother on his recent 26th birthday. He noticed once more that in the past 20 hours he had gained a few hours in the time zones.

As the Boeing 767 descended for landing, the magic of the Hawaiian Islands began to infuse into Jonathan's sensibility as he stared out through the aircraft's window. Every rain-washed feature of Oahu—its Diamond Head Mountain, the surrounding ocean of deepest, purest ultramarine flecked with prancing white horses, and the high-rise buildings housing expensive hotels—stood out with stark clarity. It had been a long voyage from Los Angeles—over 2,000 miles and about five hours of traversing an endless stretch of water. But as he saw the islands appear mysteriously from the sea, he felt as if he had stepped from nowhere into a fully realized dream. Jonathan wondered whether the ancient Polynesians, who had sailed and paddled their canoes from the South Seas to these islands more than 1,000 years ago, had felt the same way.

He had read James Michener's *Hawaii* a couple of months ago and had developed an immediate fascination for the Hawaiian archipelago with its sugar- white beaches, trembling volcanic mountains, and its legends. Jonathan had been planning this holiday in paradise for a long time now, but there was always something at his office that got in the way. It was only when he finally decided that he'd had enough and that he had to get away from it all, at least for a while, that he was able to make the final arrangements. Houston, where the headquarters of the family firm were located, was both a major aerospace research and development center and a focal point for networks of gas pipelines. A great place if it was money that you wanted. But that was all, Jonathan told himself. He had never wanted money for itself nor had he hankered after the power that a large business enterprise brings with it almost as a natural appendage, as it were. Even before going to the Hawaiian Islands, Jonathan would have exchanged his oak-paneled office in downtown Houston for a shack and a stretch of beach anywhere on that bit of heaven.

As far as he remembered, this would be his first trip outside mainland. Any time he suggested or expressed any interest in visiting any other country outside America, his mother would object– her fear was some people would harm him or kidnap him even though he always had a body guard to protect him. Jonathan never liked it but as he always wanted to keep tranquility in the family - that's the kind of person he was - he did not want to create any more commotion. There was enough tension because of his father's attitude. Jonathan did not desire to create more. It was always like that. It infused his memory of his childhood and his adulthood.

As far as he remembered, he was quite happy growing up – he had all the luxuries from the swimming pool, tennis court, most expensive cars, lots of maids and servants to the dazzling huge mansion. As a matter of fact, as a teenager though he was aware of the difference between him and the poor, like all wealthy teenagers, he did not pay much attention to that. When he used to get all the attention from the people surrounding him, especially the girls, he thought how fortunate he was. He had many digital games, the most expensive electronic gadgets, many friends, expensive clothes, and an expensive car. Before he could ask for anything, his mother would provide it for him. He would get any exotic food he wanted, expensive digital phone and camera, all were within his reach. But as he grew older, he came to understand vaguely how the system of inequality functioned – why some people are so rich and why some are so unfortunate. He would wonder about that, and then, to be absolutely sure about this notion, he would go to his father for the answer. He vividly remembered what his father said to him. "When you have poverty you would be ashamed, but, on the contrary, wealth is a blessing, and the wealthy are privileged." When he asked his mother, who had a different belief and philosophy, the same question, she would explain to him, "You know giving things away for nothing is obviously very bad – don't you think so? It is not our way – because, you know, it's called socialism or welfare. Right?" She would pause for a moment then add, "Charity alone is a band-aid solution. Well, in fact - I think, the key is to get your freebies, known in Hollywood as swag, into the right hands. You give some things but in return you would demand to get something even more." Jonathan was surprised to hear his parent's explanation, and, as a matter of fact, it made him very upset.

With all that was going on, the most enjoyable time for him was when a landscaper named Bill would come to maintain the garden's new foliage with his son, Mike. Jonathan would immediately come down to meet him and have a conversation. One day, Bill came with Mike to examine the new plants he put in the garden. Jonathan greeted them, "Hi, how are you?" They returned his greeting.

Mike saw some of the electronic games left by the pool side and said, "Oh, you are so lucky. You have so many games!"

Jonathan replied, "I don't care. If you want, you can have it." Mike played for few seconds with enthusiasm and then gave it back. Then he said cheerfully, "I am going with my dad and uncle on a fishing trip next Saturday. Dad said I have to get up very early in the morning." At that moment, Jonathan wished if he could go along with them. It would have been very adventurous and a thrilling time for him.

"I wish I could go with my dad like you do."

"Why don't you?"

"My father is always busy with his work. He has no time for me or my brother," Jonathan admitted sadly. For his 12$^{th}$ birthday, Mike went to McDonalds first and then bowling. Jonathan had to go to W Astoria where he met his father's business acquaintances and their sons and daughters, who were very well-dressed and well-behaved. The most fun he had was playing with each other's expensive electronic gadgets. "What kind of fun is that?" he wondered.

As soon as his mother found out that Jonathan was talking to Mike, she urged Jonathan to leave. To her it was inappropriate to have a conversation with a blue-collar worker. Jonathan went to his room sadly, and from the window he watched Bill and Mike laugh and chat together happily. He had never had that experience with his father.

Life's simple pleasures were forbidden to him. He could never dribble a ball on the sidewalk or ride a bicycle on the side street by himself. Jonathan was not permitted to express any dissatisfaction. That was the culture of his family. Everybody was polished, well-dressed, and subdued. Any sudden expression of sadness or joy would be an embarrassment. That's what happened one day to Jason when he was laughing loudly with his friends. His mother ordered him to leave. "Jason, you are wanted by your father." Jason understood the implications and kept quiet afterwards. With all these restriction Jonathan was often embarrassed by his enormous wealth and wished he could keep it a secret.

It was not uncommon for a rebel to be produced within the rank of an aristocratic family, and his healing thoughts would emerge from proudly insular background. He remembered when he was in high school always being surrounded by all the beautiful girls. He never played football since his mother was afraid that he would be injured. But the irony was he understood later that his wealth was the real attraction for those girls. Jonathan wanted to earn the admiration from his own effort, but everything was bought or came easily even before he wanted it or earned it.

He remembered when he was growing up wanting to explore artistic integrity. He wanted to play guitar like a rock star. Instead, he had to play piano even though he had no talent because it was more sophisticated by his mother's standard. There were many incidents like this. To his family, everything was measured in terms of money and status. His mother would say, "We have to keep our position in the society, and that's the most important thing in the world."

More often now, melancholy would set in for Jonathan about this lifestyle. To get away from it all, he finally decided to go to Hawaii. He hoped that would bring some adventure in his life and take away all the blues. He arranged everything within a day. Since his parents were on vacation, he did not have to argue with his mother.

"It was so easy to slip back", Jonathan thought as he watched the runway come into view. He could feel his hands tense, and in his mind he was manipulating the controls, reaching for the switches, his eyes scanning the dials, looking for the signals. Flying had once been a great passion.

Perhaps it would always be a passion, although lately he was caught up in sailing. In a modern airplane—even a single-engine one—you were cocooned and felt neither the wind nor the cold. On a sailboat, no matter how luxurious, you were always in direct contact with the elements, and that was what made the difference for Jonathan.

It was this new passion that triggered his interest in the ancient Polynesians and their incredible 2,000-mile journey across the open Pacific from their home in the Marquesa Islands to the Hawaiian Islands more than 1,000 years ago. Of the men who had met that vast ocean on its own terms and conquered it at a time when the most adventurous of sailors elsewhere in the world did not dare to venture more than 100 miles beyond known shores.

Jonathan looked out of the window beyond the runway that ran parallel to the one that was speedily coming up to meet his aircraft, to the vast expanse of lush land and blue water on which the Honolulu International Airport was located.

— — —

What struck him as he stepped into the main lobby were the tropical plants that grew so luxuriantly in the warm, bright, and moist air, almost numbing the senses and the tremendous diversity in the racial origins of the people that milled around in the terminal. Polynesian, of course, but there were large numbers from the Orient—Japanese, Chinese, Koreans—the Portuguese and the expected Americans.

The airport was filled with the noise of many tourists. Some of them were shouting and greeting each other; some were trying to negotiate with the flower girl to have a particular flower; some were kind of lost and looking to locate the families, friends, or the designated drivers. Another time, it would have been annoying for Jonathan to hear so much screaming - loud ear-piercing, high-pitched noise- but today it felt musical to his ear, and he was so overwhelmed with the new adventure of a new country with warm hospitality.

He walked past the Space Museum and the shops, taking note of the ubiquitous Pizza Hut, an ATM, and a jewelry shop and then went down the escalator and followed the signs in the wide corridor that led to the baggage claims area.

His eyes took in the throng of people who filled the place. The mixing of races over the past 200 years had produced a handsome people.

Jonathan could almost see Hawaiian women of rare beauty with coal-black eyes and olive thighs as they hula danced through his mind.

He had to remind himself that Hawaii had been for almost 50 years or so well and truly an integral part of the U.S.A., for the feeling that he was in a foreign country would not leave him—a foreign country where the exchange rate never varied and where the exotic natives spoke his language in addition to their own.

Once out of the airport, the air was perfumed with the heavy scent of tropical flowers. Jonathan paused and breathed in the fresh air that wafted in on the sea breeze as he waited for the taxi to roll up. The driver dressed in a bright shirt of yellow with large orange flowers, smiled broadly and said, "*Aloha!*"

Jonathan smiled back and repeated the greeting, wondering to himself why it was that people in the islands, at least the islands in the tropics, were invariably friendlier than those on the mainland. It must be something in the air.

Although he invariably stayed in the best hotels, particularly the ones with a heritage, he preferred to explore new places on his own. So, after telling the driver to proceed to the Sheraton Royal Hawaiian Hotel, he sat back to take in the scenery that flashed past the car's windows. The brightly colored flowers that grew in thickest and the lush trees that spilled over on to the road brought to mind the brochures and National Geographic magazines that he had pored over the last year.

As they passed through downtown Honolulu, he realized that the city was no different from any other American city that had gone through a building boom. In less than half an hour, the taxi drew up before a pink building of coral stucco with a distinct Moorish-Spanish design. Jonathan paid off the taxi and after the bellhop had collected his bags, proceeded to the lobby where, to his delight, he was greeted by a young woman who garlanded him with orchid lei. The true Aloha spirit, Jonathan thought to himself as he signed the register in that venerable hotel -he remembered reading somewhere that it had been inspired by the Rudolph Valentino films of the 1920s -and then allowed the bellhop to lead him to his accommodations in the Pool Tower. It was a lovely suite, and the view from the *lanai* was fantastic, offering splendid views of the ocean against the backdrop of Diamond Head, the extinct volcano, so named by early British sailors who having found volcanic crystals there thought that they had found a diamond lode.

It was early afternoon, and Jonathan could not wait to get on to the beach. The Waikiki Beach was just a step away from the hotel and after putting his stuff away, he grabbed a towel, donned the complimentary slippers, and went down to the beach where he threaded his way through a maze of umbrellas, sand castles, and bronze bodies to the water's edge. He took off his slippers on the beach and could feel the warm sand on his bare feet, giving him a warm roasting feeling. The huge waves and the ocean was so inviting he could not wait to jump in it and enjoy the luxurious swimming.

The swim was very refreshing, but after lying on the beach alone for a while he did not like the feel of the place, which getting crowded. Even the overpowering presence of beautiful women with short bikinis did not make any impression on his mind at this moment. He had read somewhere that Waikiki had once been the exclusive preserve of Hawaiian royalty and that the present generation of Hawaiians had turned it over to the tourists! He would prefer to go over to Ala Moana Beach a few miles away he thought to himself.

As he was thinking of leaving, he felt a shadow on his face and opened his eyes. Before him stood a handsome young Hawaiian man. He was more than six feet tall, weighed about two hundred pounds, and his muscles rippled in the sunlight as if smeared with coconut oil.

"You doan go surfboard?"

"What did you say?" Jonathan asked, not understanding his accent.

The young man smiled and then said, "I guess you are from the mainland. So, come on, we could go to the water for surfing."

Jonathan wanted to consider the young beach boy's proposal as he looked toward the sea at the beach boys who danced on their massive Malibu boards as they rode the surf. He was tempted, but resolutely shook his head as he was afraid that without practice he may have forgotten how to surf.

"What's the matter?"

"Nothing. I don't want to go."

"Come on, I will teach you to surf. I hope you are not afraid," he teased Jonathan with a humorous voice.

At the young Hawaiian's persistent requests, Jonathan went near the water's edge. Jonathan touched the water and did not know what came over him. Without fear, Jonathan went surfing with the native Hawaiian man. He felt free like a fish, no obstacle, no binding.

— — —

The next day, donned in cotton slacks and a colorful tee shirt, Jonathon came down to the lobby, deposited his keys at the reception desk, and went out of the hotel through the arched openings that led to the lush landscaped garden. Jonathan could smell the salted lazy air mingled with the heavy scent of oleander and large, red, yellow hibiscus. These heavy scents mesmerized his senses.

"How wonderful it is to be here, away from work for couple of days" he thought. Then he went through Royal Hawaiian Shopping Center that separated the hotel from Kealakekua Avenue, through the colorful International Marketplace with its huge banyan tree, past cart after cart, each one displaying items of jewelry that seemed to be identical that of the other.

"You'd think that so many people selling basically the same things would mean that no one would do well," he thought to himself, but then realized that he must be wrong because the carts were piled high with goods that must easily have cost a few hundred dollars.

He walked all the way to the zoo and the Kapiolani Park where he paused for a while taking in the sweep of food stands that greeted him and the smell of macadamia nut-crusted French toast that wafted towards him. He tried the delicacy—"oh it is so delicious." He was

*In Pursuit of Love, Spirituality and Happiness*

happy that he tried it. It was really good. Then he turned back and headed for the hotel enjoying the scent of the *plumeria* and the sizzle of *mahi-mahi* on the beach. That was wonderful. The heavy scent of flowers in the air, the noise of huge waves, the warm sand under his bare feet, and the friendly people with colorful clothing—all were making an imprint on his mind. He was glad that he'd taken some time off from stereotype work of Houston.

As he headed back to the hotel he heard a carillon strike up a haunting tune and looked at his watch. It was ten minutes past six. He had corrected the time before landing and so was certain that his watch was set to local time. Why then was the carillon ringing 10 minutes late? Was that the way life moved on these islands, at its own slow pace? He did recall someone saying that "Hawaiian Time" meant being late!

It turned out to be an enjoyable outing, listening to the coconut palms rustling in the wind and seeing the red ginger and flowering plumeria. Jonathan was greeted at each intersection by baskets of riotous flowers hanging from Victorian streetlamps, as he walked past hundreds of people enjoying the evening sun and the aging chess players who lounged in sheltered verandahs.

Back in his suite he fixed himself a scotch and soda and sat on the open *lanai* waiting for the sun to go down over the horizon. And when it did, in all its amber glory, it was but enchanted luxury to sit in the perfumed air and forget that there was any other world but these islands.

– – –

Tired after the long flight, the swim, and the long walk, Jonathan woke up well past daybreak. Almost immediately, he went down to the beach and spent the next hour in the water reveling in the morning surf. A good swimmer, he threw himself into the surf and swam far out into the water. Then after a hearty breakfast, he armed himself with a map of Honolulu and walked down to Kalakua Avenue.

His destination was Bishop Museum. The Bishop Museum on Bernice Street was the first on his list for it was there that he would, he knew;

get first-hand information on Hawaii, its culture, and its maritime tradition. The museum had been established in 1889 by Charles Reed Bishop, an American banker, to house the large collection of Hawaiian artifacts and the largest Polynesian collections in the world and royal family heirlooms owned by his wife, Princess Bernice Pauahi, the last of the direct descendants of the royal line of King Kamehameha I. The Museum is linked to the world's best-known Monument of love "Taj Mahal" as it tells the story of Princess Bernice falling in love with the ordinary American banker who dedicated this museum in her name. It offered a wonderful program on Polynesian navigation and space exploration as well. He also thought it best to escape the approaching noonday sun and seek relief in the cool and dark atmosphere of the museum.

He reached the museum a few minutes before 10 am... It was a dark; three-story Victorian building constructed of volcanic rock and was set on a verdant hillside campus well off Honolulu's beaten track. Jonathan decided to go on a docent-guided tour of the treasures of the Hawaiian Hall, which began at 10. He dutifully followed the docent, a stout and cheerful lady, who guided the group through the large and impressive museum. He listened as she led them past showcase after showcase that displayed necklaces woven from generations of human hair, capes made from the brilliant feathers of now extinct birds, and centuries-old *poi* bowls. The docent talked about the migration routes that brought the first people to the Hawaiian Islands from the distant Marquesa Islands. She spoke of the role of women in traditional Hawaiian society and the changes brought about by the missionaries.

"Before the missionaries came, Hawaiian women didn't wear much clothes—it was too hot," she explained. "The missionaries came along and said, 'That is not good!' They said that they would like us to wear their clothing." She giggled as she related the story of how the *muumuu*, the Mother Hubbard dresses, found its place as the ubiquitous dress of Hawaiian women.

"The *muumuu* was originally made from *tapa*, which is beaten mulberry bark fibers. Now, of course, other fibers are used, but no Hawaiian woman will trade *muumuus* for other kinds of clothing," she added with a smile. "When the missionaries came here and found Hawaiians

*In Pursuit of Love, Spirituality and Happiness*

riding surfboards, they considered that it was not a good idea as the men were disregarding God's laws by riding the water. So they banned this sport."

"Banned it!" Jonathan heard one of the tourists remark.

"Yes they did because of their religion, and Duke Paoa Kahanamoku, who revived the sport and who was the greatest swimmer ever—he won three Olympic gold medals, you know—surfboarding would have been lost forever," she said with a sigh. A little later she said, "The missionaries banned the hula too. But that is something we can understand. To their minds, this dance represented everything that was provocative about the Hawaiian Islands but of course that was revived too later."

It was at about that time that he noticed her. She was tall, almost his own height, and had long sun-shot black hair that dropped down to her waist. In her left hand, she held a notebook on which she was carefully noting down something from one of the pictures on the wall. Even from her profile he could see that she was a stunner, the pronounced eyebrows, complementing her long dark hair and her upturned nose. She was young; could not have been more than 20.

Jonathan was stung both by beauty and desire. His heart started pounding, and he felt dizzy as all the fragrances of the island came rushing in, the orchids, the pineapples, and the spray of the surf. To his mind, the lovely young woman evoked all the images that he had built up over the last couple of years about ancient Hawaii. He could almost see her on a surfboard, half-naked with her long hair streaming behind her in the wind, her lovely breasts and long legs seemingly sculpted out of amber. He could see her swaying to the languorous strains of a Hawaiian melody as she danced the hula. In his mind's eye, he could see her lead the drums to quicker and still quicker rhythms until in mounting fire her entire body quivered. And then almost imperceptibly he could feel the beat of the drum begin to slow down allowing her movements to become slow and impossibly provocative.

That was the first time ever that something like this had happened in his life. None of his adolescent crushes or the best of his love affairs would ever come close to this. He felt an inexplicable desire for possession, and he knew that this girl's sculptured face would be forever etched into his memory. Jonathan did not hear a word of the docent's patter thereafter and did not even realize that the group had moved on. He continued to stand there gazing at the beautiful young woman, dizzy from the spectacle—the wonder of her perfect figure and her pure, blossom face in profile.

It was as if the place had been made alive by her presence. After a while she became aware of his presence and slowly turned around and stared straight at him. How long had she known that he had been gazing at her, he wondered as saw her lovely face and looked deep into her dark eyes. He then smiled shyly. The beginning of love is the promise of all that is to come and it all begins with a look. Yet, although he thought that her eyes had dilated at bit—and that was invariably a sign of interest—she turned away without a response and went back to what she was doing.

Jonathan stood where he was, confident that she would turn around once more and look at him. When she did, his smile was broader than before. Her dark eyes appraised his, and for a moment there was a light in them as she rewarded him with a quiet smile. Encouraged, he moved close to her and said, "Honolulu is full of beautiful women, but you are the loveliest I have ever seen."

She did not respond except with a questioning arch of her eyebrow and an amused smile looking at Jonathan's sincere face.

"Yes, it's true," he insisted. She said nothing, as if it could be treated as a remark that needed no answer and he felt a growing sense of frustration. He wanted to say more, to make her talk, but he could not think of anything that was not silly.

They stood frozen for a moment, and then she moved away to the next display. "I'm Jonathan. Jonathan Foster. What is your name?" he asked as he extended his hand.

"Oliana, Oliana Pau," she replied as she shook his hand.

"That's a Hawaiian name, isn't it?" he asked.

"Yes. I am a *kanaka maoli*."

"*Maoli?*"

"A full-blooded Hawaiian."

"A pure Hawaiian! Were there any pure Hawaiians on the islands?" Jonathan wondered. He knew that ever since Captain James Cook discovered the Hawaiian Islands in 1778 and until the missionaries arrived in 1820 and for quite a while thereafter, the *kanakas* with their uninhibited lifestyle and legendary hospitality had given comfort to many lonely sailors who arrived in these islands. Even though the missionaries with their strict Calvinist code of behavior managed to stop everything possible to prevent polygamy, the Hawaiians never really came to terms with that. And when the diseases broke out, which had previously been unknown to the *kanakas*, and decimated the Hawaiian population from almost half a million to about a tenth of that number, there were very few pure Hawaiian left. Later, when Chinese, Japanese, and Filipino labor was imported into the islands to work on the sugar cane and pineapple plantations, there were the inevitable interracial alliances and marriages. It was therefore almost impossible for anyone to be a pure Hawaiian. Oliana's features too, though essentially Polynesian, gave some hint of other bloodlines. Her skin tone, too, was tawny enough to give a suggestion of European or other blood, which of course she was not aware of. Jonathan did not say anything, but left his question unvoiced, but she must have felt it hanging in the air for she said, "I am descended from *ali'is* who can trace their ancestry to King Kamahemeha the Conqueror of the Islands," she said proudly.

That of course was far more believable. He knew that if what James Michener had written was true, the children of some of the *ali'is*, the island chiefs, had married white men. It was therefore possible to be a direct descendant of an *ali'i* without being a true blood *kanaka maoli*. But this was just the opening of conversation he was hoping for, and he grabbed it. Without giving any thought, he engaged in a conversation.

"Although I arrived here only yesterday, I have been a student of Hawaiian culture for a few years back and I've been particularly impressed with the tremendous achievements of the Hawaiian navigators."

"Yes they were great sailors, perhaps the greatest ever."

"I agree. That's why I came here to this museum to find out more about the Polynesian sailors and their culture."

"Yes, this museum has almost every artifact that you could think of and from all over the Pacific. But it doesn't tell the whole story."

"Why do you say that?" Jonathan asked.

"Till the missionaries arrived we had no written language and we relied on an oral tradition."

"Oral tradition?"

"Yes. An *ali'i* who couldn't recite his ancestry from memory had no hope in Hawaii. So they spent years memorizing their ancestry and the various branches of their family from the time of the first canoes that brought our ancestors to these islands," she replied.

"From the time of the canoes that brought your people here? That must have been well over 2,000 years ago. Is it possible?"

She said nothing, as if it could be treated as a remark that needed no reply. But then the silence of the room forced him to say, "It seems hard to believe."

"Yes, I know, but I heard it from my ancestors and my parents many times." She murmured affectionately in response. By then they had moved quite a bit and without his realizing it, they had nearly reached the exit.

"Are there any who have maintained this tradition?"

"A few have, my father knows quite a bit."

"Your father? Interesting! Could I meet him some time?"

*In Pursuit of Love, Spirituality and Happiness*

She hesitated then shook her head and he looked at her. Something in her face was shrouded, and there was a shade of embarrassment.

"My father lives in Hilo, you know the big island."

Jonathan knew that she was trying to avoid but was hoping that she would invite him to visit her father. There were some hesitations from her part, which Jonathan could understand. At the same time, Jonathan wanted to make a good impression and wanted to create some kind of impact on her mind so that she would not disagree.

By then it was almost one o'clock. He glanced at his watch and asked, "Will you have lunch with me?"

She hesitated for a moment but kept her mysterious smile without saying anything and he wondered whether she would have to be persuaded. In the end, however, it didn't take much persuasion.

# Chapter 2

The Oceanarium at the Pacific Beach Hotel in Waikiki is a most amazing place. It is the largest aquarium located in a hotel, and it takes 280,000 gallons of water to fill the three-story-high aquarium that is filled with the most exotic array of marine life—more than four hundred creatures representing over seventy species. Because of its size and the sheer number of forms of ocean life that it supports, it is no mere aquarium and has been appropriately been named an Oceanarium.

Oliana led the way in. "Although it is viewable from any of the three restaurants here, the view from the Oceanarium Restaurant, which offers largely American cuisine is the best," she said.

Jonathan had not particularly keen on American cuisine, but he had not demurred for all that he wanted was to spend as much time with her as possible.

They entered the restaurant, and he gazed in wonder at the three-story display of Hawaiian reef life. He could see colorful schools of fish sidle

*In Pursuit of Love, Spirituality and Happiness*

up to the glass. It was almost as if they wanted to see what the guests were eating.

"It's the favorite place for Hawaiians to take out of town visitors," Oliana said as she saw him gazing in awestruck wonder at the rays and other fish that circled lazily around in the huge tank.

"I can imagine why. I don't think there's another place like this in the world." Amid that splendid display they sat down and ordered the food.

"Do you realize that you fit in so well here," Jonathan began.

"Oh! In what way?" Though she understood the remark Jonathan made, she pretended that she did not have any idea. She wanted to hear in his own word from Jonathan –whatever he had to say.

"The water, those colorful schools of fish that you can see through the glass and a lovely Hawaiian girl. It all fits in so well—just perfect."

She laughed. "There are two sides to us Hawaiian girls."

"That's not unusual; most women have different facets to their personality."

"We are like our goddesses Pele, the goddess of volcanic fire and her sister Poliahu, the goddess of the snow capped mountains—fire and ice."

"I guess you are right. Man has, after all, always fashioned his gods in his own likeness. That is why your Pele and your Poliahu embody in their character the very emotions, strengths, and weaknesses that appeal to your people."

"I had not thought of it that way," she said, a little perplexed.

"It is all very well to say that God created man in his own image. In my opinion, in all likelihood it is, may be, the other way around. But tell me about your goddesses. I have read a bit about Pele, but I don't recall the other. Poliahu, did you say?"

"Yes, Poliahu. Their story is a fascinating one. a story that has all elements of drama. Sibling rivalry, thwarted love, revenge, and a feud that endures forever."

Jonathan sat back enjoying the way Oliana intoned her words and the animated expressions on her lovely face. To Jonathan, it was more than a reward.

"Tell me," he said to encourage Oliana, taking pleasure in her exquisite explanations.

"Many, many years ago, Ai-wohi-kupua, a young chief from Kaua'i went in search of a beautiful girl whom he had seen in a dream," she began. "On his travels through the islands, he was spotted by Pele and Poliahu. Both sisters promptly fell in love with Ai-wohi-kupua, and before they knew it a battle of epic proportions had broken out. It was Pele who started it. She caused Poliahu's home, Mauna Kea, to erupt. The waves of fiery lava melted the snows that capped the mountain and caused Poliahu to flee in panic. Poliahu soon recouped her strength and returned with a snowstorm so intense that it quenched Mauna Kea's fires."

"So who won the heart of the young man?"

"Neither. But the feud still goes on."

"Even now?" he asked, arching up his eyebrow in disbelief.

"Yes. Even today, Pele's home on Mauna Loa is occasionally capped with snow though its fires remain burning, deep within the volcano. And the Big Island, which is ruled by Pele, is still tormented with fiery volcanoes and trembling earthquakes."

"Sounds very good. But it's just a myth. Who believes it?"

"Well, when Mauna Loa erupted in 1880, Princess Keelikolani recited the old chants, gave offerings of silk cloth and poured brandy into the bubbling lava to appease Pele."

"And did it work?"

"Mauna Loa became calm thereafter."

"But after adopting the Christianity, all these myths would not make any sense." His voice sounded in doubt.

"Princess Keelikolani was a Christian when Mauna Loa erupted and became serene after the offerings from him," she murmured.

"You know a great deal about Hawaii's past, don't you?"

"Yes, I do. In fact I am majoring in history at the Hawaiian Pacific University and have been taking additional courses on Hawaiian history. It is what brought me to the museum this morning."

"Is your university here in Honolulu?"

"It has a campus in downtown Honolulu, not very far from the Bishop Museum. That is where I study."

"Do you live on campus?"

"No, but I live very near the campus. My home, however, is on Aloha Ahiahi."

"Aloha Ahiahi?"

"Yes, the Big Island," she replied.

"I would like to go there sometime," he said. "I've heard that it is very beautiful."

"Yes, and mysterious too. Let me now when you plan your visit. I will put you in touch with my people there." She said in an indifferent voice as she wanted to ignore the implication that Jonathan was trying to provide. They lapsed into silence as strangers do now and then when they run out of things to talk about and tucked into the food, which had by then arrived on the table. Jonathan kept looking at her every now and then mesmerized by her beauty and charm.

Oliana, too, was a little confused about her own feelings. She rarely, if ever, went anywhere with a stranger. But there was something different about this man. Clearly, he was a good looking gentleman, and he did not have the overt superiority that most men seemed to have hanging on them almost like an accessory. It was the adulation, adoration, and his deep interest in her that had attracted her and persuaded her to agree to have lunch with a perfect stranger.

He lifted his head and his eyes, liquid pools of shadowed depths of intensity, locked into hers and held them. They gazed at each other until Jonathan spotted a couple of divers in the tank and asked Oliana what they were doing there.

"Oh, it's feeding time," she said glancing at her watch. That's part of the show. They feed the fish three times a day and on Sundays they have an additional feeding time about an hour before midday."

"Yes, it is a wonderful display," Jonathan said as they watched fish of all shapes and colors teeming around the divers, "but the air tanks and masks of the divers detract from the natural beauty of the aquarium."

"That's true," she said agreeing with him.

"Someone like you would look so mechanical in a diving suit and its attachments," he said trying to draw her into a discussion by complementing her good looks.

He expected a response to that, but she was silent. She was flattered, of course, as any woman would be at the compliments that he was paying her, but the thoughts that raced through her mind about this handsome stranger had rendered her almost mute.

"I don't care much for diving, she said eventually. "Most of my time in the water is spent surfing and I can do that for the rest of my life without getting bored. As you must know, surfing is something that we Polynesians have given to the world."

"Yes, I know that. I've done a bit of surfing myself, but I'm no expert. I've heard that to be a surfer girl in Hawaii is to be the luckiest of creatures. It means you are beautiful and tanned and ready to rip. It means that you've caught the perfect wave and are on a ride that can't possibly end." He knew with these words she would be besieged, but there were no positive response from her part.

By then they had finished the macadamia-nut banana cream pie dessert and after settling the bill they left the Oceanarium Restaurant. This was a joyful overture for Jonathan—at least she came to have lunch with him, that's a good sign. Of course, Jonathan was hoping for a kiss on the cheek or holding her soft hands but it did not happen. Jonathan then thought that maybe she need more time, after all it was only the first day.

It was very hard for Jonathan to say "good bye" now since he was not sure when he would see her again. He knew that Oliana loved surfing and that it was her life. So Jonathan whispered, hoping for Oliana's positive response "I had planned to do a bit of surfing on this trip, but I don't think I will be able to handle large waves alone."

"They won't be so large on Waikiki. You should try surfing there," she said indifferently.

"Well, a beach boy suggested that I should the day I arrived here, and I did little bit."

"Well, that's good for you. What you think?"

"Then let's go back to Waikiki, we could go surfing," Jonathan suggested desperately. Jonathan felt enormous passion toward her. He wanted to hug her, kiss her but he could not do any of those as he was not sure how she felt. He took her hand instead. Oliana kept her hand with his for few seconds, and then took it away.

Jonathan could not help thinking that perhaps Oliana did not like him. With a shattered voice he said "Oliana, don't you feel any attraction for me? I feel so much enthusiasm for you—I have never felt that way for any one, believe me."

He tried to convince her sincerely. He did not want to be defeated in this venture. There was another silence then, as she turned her head away from his gaze, and looked towards the road. She answered. "It is not that, I need little bit more time to think through." At that moment, she thought of her two cousin sisters. One of them had an affair with a foreigner. Her sister was then 19 years old. She told Oliana that they were making love all the time, day and night. Oliana saw her happy with that man—who cared for her and who would not be—day and night—that joyous sex! Two years passed by. Oliana's sister was happiest of all with all the attention she was getting from him. The love affair lasted for two years. But one Sunday afternoon Oliana was studying in the porch, her cousin sister came running to Oliana's mother. She was crying and saying, "Oh, my god, he left me for another girl. I tried so hard to get him back but I am not 19 anymore. Is it my fault?" Oliana's mother tried to comfort her but it did not help. Seeing her sister crying all the time Oliana felt very annoyed with that man.

This was the first time she'd encountered about a man who left her sister. Even then she did not think that all men were like that. But when it happened a second time with her other cousin sister, she felt she could never have a relationship with a foreigner. Her second cousin was in love with a man who married her but vanished after finding out that she was pregnant with his child. They started to search for him but could not find him anywhere. Her unleashed passion only brought her heart ache. After witnessing these and hearing many similar stories from her father, how would she trust anyone, especially foreigner? How would she know that he would not leave her after making love with her? Maybe Jonathan was different than those men. She saw that in his sincere eyes and voice. She wanted to trust Jonathan but she was utterly confused. Would she give Jonathan a chance? Torn between these she mulled over his suggestion and then broke the silence by saying, "All right," to her surprise.

She could not understand herself. What had happened to her protective sheath that usually shielded her from succumbing to situations she felt unable to handle? What had happened to her instinctive apprehension for foreigner?

Jonathan hoped for a more enthusiastic response, but she was silent thereafter. He did not understand her dilemma about what was going through her mind but was patient and wanted to give her more time.

– – –

After lunch, they went on to a stretch of beach that was close to the Sheraton. There they rented a surfboard, a large one so that they could ride tandem. Oliana had at first demurred at riding tandem, but realizing that Jonathan was not an expert surfer, she agreed. Although he had surfed a few times, Jonathan had never ridden tandem. It was, therefore, a novel experience. But it was the anticipation of being in physical proximity to the lovely young woman that thrilled him more, and that started to fill him in with all kind of wild imaginations of winning her.

They climbed on the surfboard and together paddled out to where the waves were forming. In about 15 minutes, they were far out into the sea waiting for the wave. When the comber came on, they stood up one behind the other and as the board gained momentum, Oliana could feel Jonathan's hands on her shoulders. Then they were flying through the surf. Instinctively Jonathan's arms went around Oliana's waist, and she allowed herself to be enveloped by them till the crashing wave broke at last and they were treading the foamy water.

Soon they were back on the surfboard, paddling out even further than the first time. They caught a wave that rose like a sea god and rocketed them on a rushing exhilarating ride to the shore. As they charged through the churning white, they stood erect and firmly on the board, Jonathan no longer hesitant but sure and well balanced. His arms went around her waist, not for support or out the thrill of apprehension but in the ecstasy of having her close to him. She, too, allowed herself to relax and be drawn into the cushion of his arms. Even in the welter of the surf and spray, she could feel his affection against her body. And so it continued- paddling together to the outer sea, waiting there to catch a wave, and riding that exhilarating roller through the swiftness of the sea till it crashed near the shore. Their fifth ride was the best one yet. Even in the welter of the surf and spray she could feel his warmth against her body.

Although it must have only been a few seconds, it was an eternity for Jonathan, a moment that he would savor for long and when the wave finally crashed, he did not let go of Oliana, but went down together with his arms still wrapped around her. Underwater Jonathan pulled her toward him, but she pulled away. Should she yield? Should she submit? The questions hammered in her mind. But it was too late for she had turned her face to his and she found herself slipping her arms around his chest. Her mind vainly commanded her to withdraw from the strength of that forceful body but she could not. Her disobedient lips parted and allowed the tip of a tongue, tasting of nectar and brine to invade her mouth, sending endless ripples of pleasure spiraling through her body as they kissed, long and gentle, under the water till they ran out of breath and were forced to surface.

Would you like to catch another wave?" she asked as they treaded water with their arms around each other. He looked into her dark eyes and asked, "Do you want to?"

"Let's sit on the sands for a while," she replied meeting his eyes.

They walked back up the beach, hand in hand like two little children, until they reached the shade of the umbrellas.

"I hardly know how to begin, but I must tell you that I have never felt this way about anyone," he said. She looked at him gently, and said nothing. No word could express her thoughts, and he was forced to carry on. He was not sure how to play it, but felt an enormous joy. "I love you," he blurted out after a while.

"Love me? But you hardly know me!" she exclaimed, a little surprised even though she had heard such declarations before. It did not really disturb her for she had been expecting him to say something like this, but she had not thought that it would come so early into their budding friendship.

"I know all that I need to know. I've loved you from the moment I saw you," he said simply.

"No, that's impossible. Though we are both technically Americans, we come from completely different cultural and racial backgrounds."

"That may be so, but when a man loves a woman, these things don't matter much."

"They will if it goes on."

"Of course it will go on. I don't believe in one-night stands."

"Then you should know more about me."

"I know that you are a pure *kanaka*, that you swim and surf beautifully, that you live on another island. I know that you are intelligent, that you are a student of Hawaiian university and that you love to observe the ancient customs and beliefs. You are the most beautiful woman I have ever seen and your parents must be splendid people if they could produce someone as wonderful as you. And if you give me the chance I will get to know you as well as anyone could."

She laughed and laughed. Nobody had analyzed her that way before. She had been in his company for little over a day and had enjoyed every moment of it and she had had a good time at the end of the semester, something to savor over the holidays when she would be backing home on Aloha Ahiahi. At the same time his self-assuredness, with a touch of playfulness, appealed to her for there was a touch of mystery in what he thought of her. What was she to say to this man who seemed in many ways so right, yet so different from anyone she had met?

"I don't even know who you are," she said.

"You haven't given me an opportunity to tell you anything! You did not even ask. It was I who did all the asking," he protested.

"That's true," she murmured with a smile.

"Well, then let me tell you. I am from Houston and that's where I grew up. That's where my family lives. We are bankers and do many other things. Fourth generation, if you must know." He said it in one breath. He did not want to tell more as it might hinder their relationship or it might impose some doubt in Oliana's mind.

For the first time since they met she felt him emanating a bit of pride, but like everything about him it was rather understated.

"Aha, moneylenders!" she said mischievously, an impish grin lighting up her face.

"If you must put it that way, yes," he replied, a bit stiffly and then realizing that she was only teasing, grinned back at her.

"Spend some time with me and you'll get to know me as well as you could possibly know anyone. I, too, will get to know you."

"I have to get back to Aloha Ahiahi. I'll be back only when the new semester begins in January."

"Splendid! I'll come with you," he exclaimed.

"No!"

"Why not?"

She mulled over that, once again torn between pragmatism and desire. "I can't take you home," she said finally.

"You don't have to. I'll check into a hotel, but we could spend the day together. When were you planning to leave?"

"Tomorrow," she replied.

"Well, that's settled then."

"But….," she stuttered, her brown eyes flashing in denial, yet her heart all aflutter at the thought of being with this stranger.

"No buts," he insisted. "I am coming to the Big Island whether you like it or not. I've always wanted to go there and I want to be with you."

All throughout the night Jonathan dreamed about Oliana's mysterious smile and her ocean-deep eyes—the thoughts were like an addictive wine, making him more thirsty and desperate to know her better. Oliana's mystic behavior revealed a combination of surrounding playful nature soaked with spiritualistic inspirations and findings. How simple and how wonderful that was. Compared to that, Jonathan knew that his spiritual aspirations were more complex and deeper in conscious, and esoteric—needed absolute concentration and consciousness to get in touch with the universe. We not only possess intellect but also creativity, talent, aspiration, hope, and justice and most of all love and humor.

# Chapter 3

They left the next day on an afternoon flight that took them in less than an hour to Hilo, one of the two international airports on Big Island, or Aloha Ahiahi as the Hawaiians call it. World famous for its orchids, Hilo stands where the Wailuku and Wailoa rivers empty into a very large curving bay. It was also Oliana's home town, and, at her suggestion, Jonathan had booked a room at the Bay House, a quiet, cozy, and pleasant place, a mere 10 minutes away from the airport and walking distance to everything downtown. At the airport, Jonathan rented a Grand Cherokee and they drove to the Bay House. It was a lovely place filled with the fragrance of jasmine and oleander. He noted with appreciation that it was right on the bay and that the guest rooms had separate entrances.

After checking out his room and stowing his bags, he drove Oliana to her home. It was a small but modern home, no different from any home of that size in a suburb on the mainland. There was nobody around and

Oliana let herself in with a key she had in her shoulder strap. Jonathan followed her in and was at once impressed with the manner in which the drawing room had been arranged, the way the Hawaiian artifacts blended so well with the contemporary design of the house.

"Didn't your mother know you'd be coming home today?"

"Yes, she knew, but she's at work. She has a small souvenir store where she puts in long hours, depending on the tourist season." She smiled humorously and then she teased. "It's not as if it's the first time I'm home from university."

"I guess that's true," he murmured.

He waited in the living room while Oliana picked up her bag and went up the stairs to her room. She came down a few minutes later and flounced down on the sofa. There was a note on the side of the coffee table. Oliana picked it up and started to read. The note was addressed to her from her father.

"Sorry I could not stay to greet your friend—I had to go to perform fire ring dance for the audience—tourist season, you know." Oliana looked disappointed, her father always had so little time for her, always busy with driving excursion buses or entertaining the tourists since he worked for the department of tourism. These constant absences of her father from her childhood made Oliana more drawn to herself, more imaginative in her mind and frugal.

"What are you going to do?" he asked.

"Well, I guess I'll wait for mom. Maybe she'll come home in a couple of hours."

"It's still rather early. Let's go somewhere," Jonathan suggested as he got up.

Oliana was tempted to tell him that she had to stay to talk to her mom, but she resisted.

"All right," she said rising to her feet and following him through the door and out of the house.

*In Pursuit of Love, Spirituality and Happiness*

They drove around for a while along the coast. Oliana chattered constantly and Jonathan let her talk on, enjoying the sound of her soft musical voice and sensual movement of her attractive lips.

"Aloha Ahiahi is a young island. It's still in the process of building. That's why its coastline is rugged and in many places hard to reach. But there are lots of small beaches tucked away in hidden coves. You can't take a car there but a four-wheel drive such as this will do," Oliana said as she directed him off the road and up a dirt track.

The Cherokee bounced along the track for a while until it reached a steep incline and Jonathan had to engage the special low gear. The jeep climbed slowly but effortlessly. Soon they were over the rise and before them lay a small but lovely stretch of white sand. There was not a soul to be seen. Jonathan braked to a stop in the shade of an outcrop of rock.

He took off his shoes and stepped out on to the beach. He realized that the beach was sand, as he had thought at first sight, but of crushed shell and coral.

Oliana came around the Cherokee and stood near him. The evening was fast approaching, and although, being on the eastern side of the island they could not see the setting sun, it was all the same a beautiful scene.

"Isn't it lovely?" she asked, her hand resting softly on his arm and her head on his broad shoulder. "The ocean caresses the beach daily leaving remnants of its inner beauty for us to find."

"Beautiful," he intoned captivated by the idyllic beach and its aura of exclusivity.

"Why isn't there anyone else here?"

It is not easy getting here. Imagine climbing over those rocks to get to a beach when there are ever so many other lovely beaches all over the island. There are no lifeguards either."

"Is it safe for swimming?" Jonathan asked.

"There's a saying: 'Never turn your back on the Pacific.' But there's a reef out there that protects the beach and makes it safe for swimming and snorkeling even during these winter months."

"I wish we had brought our swim wear," he sighed.

"Well, maybe we could still touch the water with our feet," she smiled and pushed Jonathan in a playful manner. Jonathan enjoyed her sweet touch.

"What I meant of course was that we could swim in our underwear," he replied with a mischievous smile knowing that Oliana would never agree. With a hoot of joy they rushed into the water up to the ankle and began cavorting there. But the water was not warm and with the sun having lost its daytime intensity, they felt the chill each time they came up out of the water.

"Gosh, it's cold," he said through chattering teeth as they came out of the water half an hour later, into the gathering darkness.

"Yes, it is," Oliana said, hugging him gently. They ran back to the jeep and got in. Jonathan turned the engine over and switched on the heater. They sat in the Cherokee seeking the warmth of each other's bodies. Jonathan wanted to kiss her even more at that moment but was waiting for the first sign from Oliana. Oliana felt the urge too but unwillingly took her slender quivering body away from Jonathan's, which was hard. Ignoring her feelings she said, "You should come here in April. It will be warmer, but more than that, it's when the Merry Monarch Festival is held."

Jonathan was little bit disappointed but did not press it. He was willing to do anything for her even that meant for a long time to wait.

"Are you listening, Jonathan?" She asked ignoring her trembling body full of desire.

"Merry Monarch, you said?"

"King Kalakua, it was he who restored the nearly lost art of hula," she said.

*In Pursuit of Love, Spirituality and Happiness*

"Is there much to the hula other than a lot of gyrating of your hips?" he asked teasingly.

"It is an art form. At the Merry Monarch festival, hula groups come from as far away as Japan and even Europe to take part in the competition. The festival is always sold out months in advance," she said proudly.

"Competition? How can you hold competitions for something as erotic as hula?"

"Hula isn't just some kind of wild gyration. When it was started out it used to be a dance to propitiate our Gods and Goddesses. Now though for the commercial pay off it turned into a popular culture" Oliana protested.

She was miffed by Jonathan's attitude, but he was oblivious to this. "That's the general perception," she thought. Why did she not retort? She wondered. Was she trapped by her own heart, and in a manner she had never imagined? She had no answer to her own question. There was a fire burning inside her and she thought of the volcanoes on the island—chiseled by the wind and pounded by the waves. Of the towering lava walls bejeweled with emerald green and silver threads of water—a marriage of forest and falls.

"Mind of mine," she told herself. "Hear the mountains calling for peace and solitude, for insight and wisdom, for courage and strength. What am I going to do?"

After a while, Jonathan suggested that they should go back to the Bay House where they could have a bath and change into something comfortable. Oliana was lost in reverie and it took a while for the suggestion to register. When it did, she nodded her head in agreement. Jonathan engaged gear and then drove up over the ledge of rocks. She was silent for most part of the ride, thinking about his casual response to hula dancing, which was not very new to her. She had been attracted to him from their very first meeting yet it felt that it had been so sudden, she recalled. She had felt his intense gaze upon her and turned around and then he had looked away from her. Of course it was his good looks that had first attracted her, but then when he spoke she had become aware of his grace, courtesy, and his inherent goodness. Within days it had become so strong that it was almost frightening in its intensity. Yet she found some of his attitudes disquieting and it was only when they had entered his room that she broke out of her reverie once more to say, "I must call my mother and let her know I'll be home soon."

And she did immediately, before he had time to suggest that she should have dinner with him. He waited while she had a shower, listening to her love humming a tune. She soon came out wearing his bathrobe which he offered. When he had had a shower himself, they sat on a couch on the lanai, listening to the gentle sound of the surf pounding on the beach below. He smiled and tried to take her in his arms and her heart hammered slightly whether from the smile or the obvious pleasure he found in her company, she did not know. The smell of him, the feel of him was boldly male. But she pulled away gently and he did not pursue it. Lots of things were going through her baffled mind.

She might wrap her arms around him while cavorting in the water or on the beach, he knew, but there was something holding her back, as if she was infected by some edgy combination of apprehension and longing. She had to be pursued and won. Tonight he had to let her just be.

"We must go to the Hawaii Volcanoes National Park. It is truly unique for there's no place like it anywhere in the world. You can't visit Aloha Ahiahi without a good look at it," Oliana said after a while.

"Yes, I saw something about it in the flight magazine," he volunteered.

"Imagine flying over the most active volcano on earth, a volcano that is erupting right now."

"Erupting at this very moment!" he exclaimed.

"Yes, and it has been ever since 1983."

"Isn't it dangerous to go there?" he asked.

"Not now. My mother still remembers it shooting a fountain of lava several hundred feet into the air. It was at about midnight and it lit up this house like it was daytime. But these days it is much more sedate."

"But it still erupts, doesn't it?"

"Yes, it does, but not significantly in the last few years. Most of the lava goes out to the sea through underground tubes. Even so, they say that on an average day the volcano pumps out several hundred thousand cubic yards of lava."

"Isn't that's dangerous for someone who goes there?"

"The park is huge. It covers about 13 percent of Aloha Ahiahi."

"That's a lot of territory," he observed.

"We can go to the crater's edge, but to really see the place you must fly over the park."

"We'll do that," he agreed. "But I thought you had suggested driving there?"

"Yes, it's only 30 miles from here and we will go by car. But to really see the volcano and the effect it has on the surrounding area you should take a flight."

She was quiet after that. There was something in the pit of her stomach. Was that love? Her spirit had long searched for a love as stable and as giving as the ocean. Would this man who she had loved almost from the moment she had seen him be able to give her that, she wondered. It was a new experience for her for in these matters. She had long been used to being in control of the situation.

Here, however, his power over her seemed to be growing stronger and she was no longer sure of her feelings. But she hid these emotions and suggested that it was time for her to go home. Jonathan could not show his disappointment but merely smiled at her and did as she had requested. He made her promise, however, to come to the Bay House the next day.

--- 

Jonathan was waiting anxiously the next day, and every few minutes he looked at his watch. On the dot of 10 he heard a knock on the door.

"I've been waiting for you for a long time. For a moment I thought you wouldn't come," he said drawing her into his arms restlessly and planting the passionate kisses on her lips for a long time. Little did he know—Oliana had been waiting to come since 9 o'clock. She hardly slept. Was it a dream? They stayed in that position, hugging, kissing, and touching each other's bodies over and over again to get to know each other from the beginning, refreshing their exhausted memory. Finally she sat down on a chair on the lanai burdened with all the draining passion and asked in her usual soft, musical voice, "What would you like to do today?"

"Let's fly over the volcano. You wanted to do that before." Jonathan suggested.

"Yes, that should be fun," she agreed.

Soon they were off to a private airfield nearby where they boarded a helicopter that took them on a flight over the park. It took them right over the crater of Kilauea and they were able to look right into that gaping maw and see the molten lava spilling out over the lip of the crater, from where it flowed like a river down the slope of the mountain. It was a fascinating sight; a bright and glowing river that slowly ran down to the sea. There were also other breakouts on to the surface, which had widened the flow towards the east.

"That's a great deal of lava," Jonathan was surprised.

"Yes, but there's even more being produced," Oliana told him.

"More? Yes, of course, the underground tubes, I imagine" he responded.

"This is Pele's home."

"Ah, the goddess of volcanic fire. Surely you don't believe all that stories?"Jonathan asked.

Oliana did not reply and Jonathan was too caught up in the sight of that spectacularly active volcano that he did not see her crestfallen face. 'I wonder what you'll say when you find out how I feel?' she asked silently. They also saw puffs of white fume rising from the ground and

*In Pursuit of Love, Spirituality and Happiness*

when she saw his questioning look, Oliana told him, "That's steam breaking out through cracks in the underground tubes." Further on, out at sea, they could see a plume of white smoke.

"That's what happens when the boiling lava hits the water." Jonathan did not speak for a long time, even after the helicopter had brought them back to the airfield. It was as if the raw power of nature had stilled his tongue. Nature does sustain the condition what already was created but could not create it by itself, he thought. A few weeks ago, Jonathan was just a visitor on the Hawaiian Island, an adventurous American young man who had never been engaged in any deep thought. After meeting Oliana, things started to change and he was involved in trying to analyze everything surrounding him, including Oliana's deep sense of nature with its wrapped intensity of mysticism including Pele. It seemed like she derived her life from the nature—the ice-capped mountains and the exotic volcanoes. It invaded her when she was a little girl and made her blossom in her youth.

Sensing the need for a pause, Oliana kept quiet, too. But after a while she tried to bring him out of that somber mood.

"I can stay here for a long time but I think you looked tired Jonathan from all this smoke and lava. Let's go back to the Bay house" she suggested. After returning from the trip Oliana changed into a slick long gown. She took some pillows from the bed and put them on the balcony and sat on them. Jonathan flopped down by her side. Jonathan gazed at her tenderly. She, too, seemed moved by the wonder of the moment—the orange flame of the darkening sky, the pristine beach that the ocean washed hour upon hour erasing forever all its mistakes and leaving it in a fresh new state.

She sat beside him, happy to have him there, and watched the horizon. She had quite enjoyed the days that she had spent with him. A mood of drowsy content held her. It was as if like spring giving way to summer, reassurance had strengthened her friendship with Jonathan.

Before Jonathan went out for the trip with Oliana, he made all the arrangement to surprise Oliana, to indulge, to show how passionate he was about her. Jonathan made a request to the hotel's maid service to arrange a bubble bath and to light the candles all over the bathroom to display a glimmer of shadow and light. The previous night, he bought the most exquisite gardenia perfume that she adored. With his surprise what he had never done before for anyone, he placed the pink orchid pedals all the over the exquisite bathroom floor for Oliana. It was another of her favorite flowers that thrived in the mild and pleasant climate and volcanic cinders of Hilo.

After staying for a while on the balcony with Oliana, he asked her to close her eyes and then took to the beautiful bathroom. At his request Oliana opened her eyes. "You can walk on the floor now, Oliana. The orchid's pedals would touch your feet—I wish I was those orchid pedals," he said in a poetic voice. Oliana's eyes broadened with surprise. "All those for me?" Fire of love melted her heart. She'd waited for that moment for a long time, and finally it came true. When they were in the Jacuzzi, the air was filled with Oliana's favorite perfume; Jonathan smiled and gave her a bunch of jasmine flower to place on her hair. Soft music played in the background.

Oliana said, "Hold me tight." Jonathan was overwhelmed with her response. Holding her tight on his broad chest Jonathan said, "You came to my life like rain. You have completely changed my life. Now I know that my life has a meaning; now I know what it means to be in love." Then without hesitation Jonathan gave Oliana's lips a passionate, long kiss. Oliana slipped into heaven. The fire of love melted her away.

All of a sudden, a thought arose in Jonathan's mind as if Oliana were not there anymore. That empty feeling haunted Jonathan for a moment. He squeezed Oliana even tighter to his chest. Jonathan enjoyed this heavenly moment so much that he wanted it to last forever. She too surrendered herself to this man's spontaneous passion and with a glance of admiring eyes she said to Jonathan, "I want it last forever, too, Jonathan."

Afterward, they came out of the water and Jonathan said, "Let me dance with you." Some water was still dripping through Oliana's clothes, and Jonathan could clearly see Oliana's beautiful young breasts. Another time Oliana would have objected to that proposal, but nothing mattered any more. Cheek to cheek they danced for a while—long simmering desire turned into a deep sensual passion.

The evening sky was sparkling with many shades of glitter, some deep red and some light red, enchanting. The sun was setting to the west, reminding the night is near. Oliana said, "I do have to go back home."

"After dinner" said Jonathan. He didn't want to let her go so soon. They spent a while driving around, until Jonathan spotted a convivial and expensive-looking restaurant.

"That looks rather nice. Let's have dinner there," he suggested. Jonathan was in an expansive mood and ordered a bottle of the most expensive champagne and when it arrived and the cork had been popped, he did not allow the waiter to pour it out. He poured it into one of the flutes and saying, "I love you Oliana" put the crystal to her lips, yet holding it by its stem.

When she had taken a sip, he put it to his own lips and took a sip and said, "This is a token of the way our life is going to be. We will forever sip our champagne from the same flute."

Oliana smiled at the thought. She was still torn between her attractions to this wonderful man and her inexplicable sense of foreboding, of something she could not put a finger on. She put those thoughts away as Jonathan reached for her hand and held it tenderly. He looked deep into her eyes and said, "You have the most beautiful eyes. Has someone told you that? I bet they have."

Oliana smiled and looked away, but her soft hand continued to rest in his. Jonathan spurred on by that small degree of hope, took her hand in his and pressed on.

"I love you, Oliana," he said, his quiet voice penetrating the mist that seemed to be forming in her mind. "It is not just a groin-tickling attraction. I know it. These sweet days in paradise—warm days filled with trust spontaneity and fun—have shown me that. My love will be your anchor. The strongest winds cannot tear me away from you or you from me. For if you only knew, my darling, all that I have, all that I do, I'd give it all away."

She lifted her gaze to him, her eyes suddenly shining with tears of joy as she saw the light in his eyes. Her hand was still in his, and she found his warm, firm clasp reassuring. It was truly unbelievable how he had taken her breath away from the very first day when she had seen a smile on his face. And now he had bared his heart to her in a way no one had before. She was no longer filled with doubts and fears about his intentions and the future.

# Chapter 4

The next day they decided to go in the Cherokee to the Volcanoes Park. They set out early in the morning and drove the 30 odd miles up Highway 11 to the park. The land rose steadily past macadamia orchards, abandoned sugarcane, and rain forests until they reached the park. There they stopped at the Kilauea Visitor Center and crossed the road to the Volcano House Hotel, an old style country lodge, and parked the Cherokee in its parking lot.

"It is a very old hotel," Oliana said.

"Yes, it does have an old world look about it."

"It was first a grass hut and that was more than 150 years ago. Then about 20 years later, a more substantial building of grass and *ohia* poles was made. Later a wooden building was erected. The fact remains that the fireplace in this hotel has had a fire burning for the last 125 years!" she exclaimed proudly.

"That is some tradition," Jonathan agreed. They left the parking lot and walked the few hundred yards to look at the Kilauea caldera.

"It is huge!" Jonathan exclaimed.

"Yes, it's almost two miles across and at least five hundred feet at it's deepest." Further on they could see Mauna Loa.

"That is the world's most massive single mountain," Oliana told him as they gazed up at the huge mountain that rose to over 30,000 feet. (It's only about 13,000 feet high?) They returned to the parking lot, got into the Cherokee, and drove clockwise around Kilauea's rim and soon entered a rain forest of ferns and red-blossomed *ohia* trees and paused at the Kilauea Iki Crater.

"Would you believe that as recently as 1959, this was a lake of boiling lava with fountains that went up to almost 2,000 feet?"

"Well, all that you can see now is a steaming black crust. Funny thing about volcanoes, they start out beautiful, and then…poof!"

"You can imagine the power of Pele."

"You really believe in this Madame Pele?" He was still wondering about Oliana's strong belief. "Yes. She is the personification of female power."

"That I can understand. They start out beautiful and then….," he said with a mischievous smile.

"Well, her story is a fascinating one and you must listen to it to understand my feelings about it. Long ago, before man knew how to make fire, a baby girl was born to Haumea, the Earth goddess and Moemoe. She was one of six daughters and seven sons and was the one who her wise uncle foretold would bring them fire. Her name was Pele. Time passed and she grew into a beautiful young woman and like her uncle had foretold, she brought them fire. But this gift soon became a problem, for she kept setting things on fire and because of this she and her sister Namakaokahai, an ocean goddess, got into many fights. Finally, it became a fearful row and Pele was chased out of her homeland in Kahiki."

*In Pursuit of Love, Spirituality and Happiness*

"Kahiki?" Jonathan asked.

"Yes, Kahiki. Kahiki means any place that is out of sight."

"All right." He nodded his head.

"Well, Pele first went to Lehua, a small volcanic cone sticking up out of the water. It's just north of Nihau. Fire is the essence of Pele and she tried to dig into the island but was unsuccessful and so went on to Western Kauai. From there she went from island to island chased by Namakaokhai. Finally she came to Big Island where she began digging down with her *paoa*, a magic spade. At last she found fire, and since then she has made her home here."

"A fascinating tale," Jonathan said.

By then they had reached Halemaumau Crater, an impressively steaming crater.

"The story doesn't end there. Pele was sleeping in her home here in this crater when she heard the sounds of a hula festival. Using her powers of astral travel she followed the sounds to Haena on Kauai. There she saw a handsome chief Lohiau dancing at the festival and fell head over heels in love with him. She changed her form to that of a beautiful young woman and entered the dance and captured the heart of the young chief. She lived with him for a while and then when she had to return home she left promising Lohiau that she would send for him."

"She could have taken the fellow with him," Jonathan said with a bemused smile.

"Whatever you may say, the site of Lohiau's house and the ruins of the temple where Pele danced with Lohiau is still there on Kee Beach on Haena."

"Granted. But what happened to the lovers? That's what interests me."

"For reasons unknown to us Pele could not return to Haena and sent her sister Hi'iaka to bring Lohiau back to her island."

"The eternal triangle," Jonathan murmured.

"No! To ensure that she did bring Lohiahu back, she threatened that she would kill Hi'iaka's friend Ho'poe if Hi'iaka did not return in 40 days with Lohiau. When Hi'iaka reached Kauai she found Lohiau dead. She immediately rubbed his body with herbs and chanted magical intonations and in time brought Lohiau back to life. Lohiau was grateful and agreed to accompany her to Aloha Ahiahi."

"And they lived happily ever after?"

"No. Unfortunately the 40 days were over by then and Pele suspected that Hi'iaka and Lohiau had fallen in love and were not coming back. She became furious and in her rage she caused an eruption that turned Hopoe to stone. When Hi'iaka reached Aloha Ahiahi and saw her friend as a statue in stone, she decided to take revenge. She led Lohiau to the very edge of the Halemaumau crater where Pele could see them and there embraced the young chief. Pele flew into rage and the volcano erupted covering Lohiau in lava and flame."

"She's a nasty piece of work," Jonathan suggested with a smile.

"Not really. She brought Lohiau back to life and confident that she would choose her, asked him which sister he loved. Lohiau, however, chose Hi'iaka."

"Did she kill them both?"

"No, she blessed them and allowed them to sail back to Kauai."

"Oh. That seems out of character."

"Perhaps, but the smell of sulphur reminds us that she is still living here."

"I have no faith in anything supernatural." Jonathan declared.

"If you can believe the Biblical stories of Moses parting the Red Sea, or of Lot's wife being transformed into a pillar of salt, why can't you believe this story?"

"Well, it is something to do with the miracle, so we believe it. But if you think that story of Pele make sense to you that's all right with me."

Jonathan knew now that Oliana really believed in it with her heart.

"Well, what do you think of this? Do you think that Pele's route through the islands followed the progression of volcanic activity in geological time would not count for something?" Oliana wanted to convince Jonathan in her own terms and validate how she felt.

"I believe, that, then, these events have happened over a period of thousands of years and for a people to know the order in which these events took place, so to you it should not appear to be at all supernatural. That is why even today you have people who come here and dance the hula on the crater's edge in homage to Pele."

"Perhaps, but that's something I have always wanted to do as I believe," she said.

"Dance on the rim of the crater, with boiling lava below?" he teased Oliana.

Oliana lapsed into silence thereafter and Jonathan sensing her hurt did understand that it was too precious for Oliana. Jonathan looked again at Oliana and said, "I am sorry if I hurt your feeling, Oliana. Now I understand how you feel and we all believe in something. I am really sorry." After sensing the sincerity in his voice, Oliana kissed him. Jonathan leaned on the railing of the lanai and stared out at the dark ocean below.

After the trip, Jonathan sat near Oliana. She tried to ward off her awareness of how close he was to her. She was conscious of his body and its warmth, even before he touched her. His hands overlapped across the front of her stomach, his fingers spreading across her rib cage below her breasts. It started quicksilver fires that flamed through her limbs and left her with an aching tension that twisted her stomach into knots. Her hands crossed each other to seek his wrists. When they found them, they could only hold them in the same position. The thought of removing them fled the moment her fingers felt the wisps of masculine arm. Her sensitive nerve ends vibrated with the sensual contact. Jonathan's head bent toward her, his jaw and chin brushing near her ear, his warm breath stirring the silken texture of her skin. His male scent masked by the fragrance of the fresh yet elusive cologne set her heart tripping wildly against her ribs. She closed her eyes against the quickening reaction of her senses to him, but it only served to increase his ardor.

The thought of him was dominating her mind. There wasn't room for anything else for he crowded into every nook and cranny of her being, dominating it until she could only shake her head in dazed protest as his mouth explored the side of her neck, sending delicious shivers over her sensitive skin. He nuzzled her ear, his teeth gently nipping at the lobe. The caress unleashed a torrent of reactions. She melted against him, his frame more sharply defined against her curves. An arm was removed from around her as his mouth lingered near her ear and then moved away.

A second later he was lifting her off the couch. When he did that, her hand automatically curved around his neck as he sat her down, cradling her on his lap. A fine-boned tension was making her hold herself stiffly in his lap. She kept wondering if she was too heavy or if he was comfortable in this position. His dark blue eyes watched her as he slid his fingers down her hand, his thumb rubbing the inside of her wrist and making exciting forays to her sensitive palm.

His eager mouth sought her languid lips, and in the intoxicating pleasure of his possessing kisses, she became ready and her position on his lap became more natural and she began to relax for the first time since they returned to Bay House that day.

"I love you," he uttered through lips muffled by her skin and then he took out a ring and slid it on her beautiful long finger. Oliana looked at it and saw that it was engraved with a fiery volcano. She did not say anything but as the headiness of the moment gave way gradually to raw desire that spread through her veins heating her flesh to a feverish pitch, she hugged him tightly and that was answer enough for him. Nothing registered in her mind, but the aching love and ultimately desire. She shuddered in ecstasy and surrendered herself to his gentle caresses. It was too late to think about her misgivings or worry about what would come next. A second later Jonathan turned, and lifted her off the couch and carried her to the bed.

The next few days went by in a whirl. Jonathan was thrilled that he had gotten past whatever defenses she had put up. He did not know why she had been distant at times, but that did not matter anymore. "After all," he told himself, "who could really understand women."

Oliana would arrive each morning and they would go to various places of interest on the island. Most of the time Jonathan went by her suggestions without protesting. Occasionally, however, he would demur.

"We must go to Pu'uhonua 'O Honaunau one of these days," Oliana said.

"Pu'uhonua?"

"Yes, the Place of Refuge. It's another world famous site and it has been restored to almost its original condition although the size of its surrounding areas has been reduced a great deal."

"What's important about it?"

"In the old times before the *kapu* system was done away with…"

"*Kapu?*" he interjected.

"Taboo," she explained and then continued. "Those who broke a *kapu*, or enemy warriors, or anyone who was in fatal disfavor with the *alii'* or the *kapuna*, the priests that is, could take refuge here and find forgiveness. The trick was to reach it alive: you had to swim a shark-filled channel as the last step."

"How far is it?"

"It's on the other side of the island. It's about an hour by road from Kailua-Kona."

"That's quite far. Is it worth the effort?"

"Well, today it keeps alive the old ways by preserving such arts as *kapa* pounding, music and dance traditions and *lau hula* weaving. Inside the park you can go on a self-guided tour that takes in a sacred site, the

Hale O Keawe Heiau, which was built in 1650, wooden *kii* images, canoe sheds, and other ancient structures and artifacts."

"If you feel so, then I guess we should go there," he said. But they did not get around to going to any place anyway. As Jonathan would remark later to Oliana, "The only place of refuge that I want is in your arms."

For a few days the time went by fast with lots of hug, affection, sumptuous kisses, and intense love every now and then.

– – –

A few weeks ago, Jonathan would not have thought of any of these so strongly. As any young man would, he was merely enjoying the beauty and the charm that a young woman would offer him. But after spending so much time with Oliana and falling in love with her, Jonathan wanted to appreciate her. Oliana's obsession with the nature created mysticism surrounding her.

Her deep love and knowledge for her own culture attracted Jonathan and made an impact on his mind. With the verge of emotion she offered him affection, love, and in-depth knowledge, which he had never experienced before.

Jonathan had decided from the very moment he had seen Oliana that this was the woman for him. It had taken him more than three weeks from their first moments of intimacy to get her to agree to marriage. Oliana, too, had been immensely attracted to Jonathan from the moment he had approached her in the museum. That was why she had allowed herself to be wooed by a stranger; something she had not expected would finally go so far and become so intense.

There were the expected obstacles, of course. Oliana's mother was not happy at the thought that Oliana would be giving up her studies. Oliana too, did not want to give that up. That was her primary objection to a quick wedding. Jonathan, ever optimistic, did not see any problem in that.

"You can continue your studies in Houston. After all, your university does not have any course that can't be pursued in Houston. And you will be able to carry your credits, too," he assured her. These assurances gave Oliana the confidence she needed. Oliana's father who was hardly there suddenly began taking an interest in his daughter. In his youth, he had been a beach boy, who escorted the women from the mainland, taught them to surf. When age caught up with him, he began to drive a bus that took tourists all over the island. He was sure he knew what *haloes* were like and he did not relish the thought of his daughter marrying one. But clearly this man was well-to-do and absolutely sincere about his daughter, and that, of course, made a difference. Jonathan, feeling insecure and embarrassed by his diminutive knowledge of this land, wanted to know more about Hawaii from Oliana's father. Oliana's father was enchanted and thrilled.

"Living in harmony with the land was developed into an exquisite art form, and generosity in all things, especially in the sharing of food. We have a four- month First Fruits Festival called Makahiki. During the Makahiki, Lono, the God of Peace, brought fertility to the land, while the people celebrated life. Ku, the God of war, was blindfolded and left powerless, and during the four-month festival both hard labor and war were taboo. It was a Pono (righteous) life, one filled with universal harmony, and that pono was maintained so long as the Ali'I Nui, or high chiefs, followed the advice of their religious and political leaders. The Hawaiian Gods regulated the correct phases of the moon for fishing and farming, for the building of temples and for celebration of life. The people and the land prospered as a sophisticated civilization and we, the Hawaiian, are carrying on our cultures through a tradition of hula and mele Oli (chants) full of stories of gods and goddesses, ceremonies, prayers, protocol, imagery wisdom, and intelligence. In Hawaiian mythology, the power of woman was a force that must never be ignored." Jonathan understood the implication and the cultures of Hawaii in broader term as Oliana's father was explaining the Hawaiian culture and customs.

Many ancient and traditional people perceive the nature as God and accept spirituality through it. Jonathan had no problem with that. To him God created the nature for us to feel the beauty of it and consume it and experience the wrath as nature bounded by the laws as we would be.

Another obstacle was his parents who would be most upset. How could they come to terms with having a Polynesian daughter-in-law, no matter how exotic? What would their friends at the club say! He could imagine his mother, Sophie Foster, upset and Spencer Foster ranting and raving and threatening to cut Jonathan off without a cent. All that would be to no avail for money was not an issue. Jonathan's grandfather had set up a trust fund for two of his grandchildren and, having crossed few years ago, he had access to all the income from those funds. But that was not the point. He did not want to quarrel with his family as he was very fond of them and loyal to them.

But on the other hand, he knew that whether they liked it or not, there was no going back on his decision to marry Oliana. He was so much in love that all the moments he was waiting to be married were exhausting in his mind. That's why Jonathan wanted to marry Oliana over the next few days as he could not wait any longer, and at the same time he would not have to face his parents as they were on their annual winter cruise and there was no way he could contact them until their ship reached its next port of call, wherever that was.

"Should we not wait till they return?" Oliana asked, one evening when they were in his room at the Bay House.

"There's no point in doing that," he replied.

"Why not?" she pressed on.

"Well, this is the only time my father can take the time off from work."

Actually Jonathan wanted to complete his wedding in this opportune moment as he knew that his parents would object vigorously. Though Jonathan was prepared to face any arguments from his parents, he did not want Oliana to be subject of any criticism. His protective sheath would always guard her and save her from any harm brought by any one. He drew her into his arms and kissed her, then cupped her face between his hands.

"Won't they always hold it against me? Why can't we wait till they return?"

"No! I don't want to wait, I can't wait any more. Maybe after a while, they will stop thinking about it and then it will be a forgotten chapter in their lives."

"They will forget?" she asked, raising an eyebrow.

"They are very busy people. Dad's too busy making money and Mom has her club, charity, and her circle of friends. That's all that matters to them." He could not explain to her fully as he knew that Oliana would not be able to understand the implication of the materialistic world where luminescent money and affluent status only brings out the meaning of the so-called worthy life. Tradition and mental emotion had very little value in that world. It would only distress Oliana as she was expecting so much. She would only be disappointed with his parents' response.

"Even so…"

"Well, you don't know what they are really like. I do!" he exclaimed, holding her close and kissing her on her cheek over and over and then his lips sought the curve of her mouth.

"But they are your parents!" she tried to ask emotionally one more time.

"You must know by now that I do not believe in traditions the way you do." He provided another explanation. No way would he let anyone ruin their precious marriage. She did not say a word. Her fingers trembled uncertainly against his bare chest until they began to enjoy the feel of his smooth, muscled skin. He tilted her face with his hands and settled his mouth against hers. Oliana slid her arms around him, locking herself tight against the hard column of his body. Her eyes closed and she gave herself up to the heady plunge of his tongue into the well of her mouth. Even after all the intimacy of the past few weeks, they just could not get enough of each other. Jonathan put his forehead to hers, breathing laboriously, and his heart thumping hard as if he had run for miles.

"So beautiful," he whispered, dismayed at the inadequacy of the words, "You are beautiful."

Later that night Jonathan gently removed her hand from his chest and without disturbing her made his way outside. It was as if he was in a dream - the myriad colors of the lagoon ever changing as the tall coconut palms shrugged their fronds in the purple darkness and the wind rustled through the leaves. The glimmer of the waves washing over the beach and the muted thunder of the surf beyond the reef made that scene alive and unforgettable as he stood there in the open air enjoying the luxury of the cool and refreshing breeze and the sweet sensation of precious love. This land had it all—the solitude and if you listened carefully you could feel the mysticism in the air, the enchanted active volcano would remind you the power of higher power. The hibiscus flower with fragrance and deep ocean around the island would make you feel overjoyed, and solitude mountain ranges would make you feel spiritualistic. Jonathan thought passionately for a while in that way, his sub-conscious mind made an effort to override everything what was typical, ordinary and usual. He now could understand Oliana's passion for mystic nature and spiritual aspect as he was in love with her. He remained there for quite a while and then finally went back indoors and lay down quietly by her side. That was where he would be content to be all his life, he knew.

--- --- ---

They decided to have the wedding in a garden location. Because most of these places were located in areas that could be rainy overnight, they chose to conduct it in the mid-morning.

It was a beautiful setting. Near enough to the ocean for them to hear the crashing of the surf, the garden was complete with a cascading waterfall. It was so enchanting that as they approached the white pavilion, Jonathan wondered for a moment whether the fabled Garden of Eden was something like this. That garden, if it did ever exist, must have been here, he told himself. After all, until the missionaries arrived and brought their proper ways with them, the Hawaiians had no

*In Pursuit of Love, Spirituality and Happiness*

concept of it. Clothes were a mere adornment to be worn to enhance beauty, not to hide it.

Oliana looked stunning in her long floral dress. Her beautiful tiara, bangle, and garland were made of gardenia flowers and all her relatives and friends looked ever so beautiful. The music that wafted through hidden speakers, lent an air of sublimity to the proceedings as the bridal procession made its way toward the white pavilion where a pastor stood waiting.

The broad-shouldered pastor looked at the gathering. "Let us take a moment to be aware of all the beauty around us, taking in a breath of air, and listen to the sounds of nature, as the waves come up on the shore and the gentle breezes caress our face, feel the harmony of this island," he began. "We are all part of one, and we call upon the love that is ever-present to bless this special day."

It seemed like a dream come true for Jonathan. The choir comprised largely of Oliana's cousins then intoned the age-old chant.

> *Onaona I ka hala,*
> *E ka lehua oia na ka noe O ka'u no ia, e ano'I nei,*
> *Ea li'a nei, ho'I o ka hiki mai,*
> *A hiki mai no ou kou, a hiki pu no me ke Aloha e Aloha e.*

"The "oli Aloha" says in part that, this is the sight for which you have longed. Now that you have come, love has come with you" Oliana whispered to Jonathan.

"In Hawaii we exchange *leis* as a symbol of our love," the pastor continued. "The beautifully crafted lei, with its hand-picked flowers and twine, carefully bonded together with love, are a reflection of your love and *Aloha* that you share for one another. As you exchange these *leis,* you will begin to weave your *lei* in life with love throughout eternity. May the exchange of these *leis* be the new beginning of your lives together, and now we ask for the blessings of life so we may open our hearts to the ways of love. Now, with loving *Aloha*, please present your *leis* to one another with a smile and a kiss upon each other's cheek."

They turned toward each other and, after one had garlanded the other, Jonathan put his hands around Oliana and kissed her. It was the first time that he had kissed her in public. It was a strange yet thrilling feeling. The service retained a great deal of what he was used to in a wedding service on the mainland. The vows and the exchange of rings were almost identical. Finally, after they had placed rings in each other's fingers, the pastor paused for a while and then said, "May peace and unconditional love surround you and remain with you now and forevermore. And so by the power vested in me by the State of Hawaii, I now pronounce you Husband and Wife. You may seal your vows with a kiss."

The music became a bit louder and as they turned after kissing. It shifted seamlessly to the Wedding March to which they walked down the open-air aisle with Oliana resting her head lightly on Jonathan's shoulder. Everybody enjoyed the luau. The air was filled with aroma of kalua pig—a whole young pig wrapped in leaves and roasted in a pit called an imu, chicken wrapped in plant leaves and steamed, rice and plenty of fresh fruits like banana, papayas, pineapple etc, a food lover's paradise.

In the background, Hawaiian musicians played the ukulele brought to the island by Portuguese and the steel guitar invented by Joseph Kekuku, a Hawaiian, about 1895.

It was such a beautiful ceremony, Jonathan thought, such a wonderful blend of Christian liturgy and Hawaiian chant. For a split second he wished his parents had been there to witness it. But then he pushed that thought aside. The Fosters were known for their snobbishness, and his parents would have been aghast at his wedding clothes and that of his bride. Had they come, their friends would ask to see the photographs of the wedding and they would be hard pressed, he knew, to explain what he was doing in a bright floral shirt!

Perhaps he would have dressed formally had they been there. Some American couples that got married in Hawaii did just that, he knew. But it was impossible for him to think that in this situation.

He was hoping OC would come. This was his best friend who always supported him in any circumstances, hold up for him without any interest. OC was smart, intelligent and above all a quick thinker and very honest. Jonathan always used to think that he was very lucky to have a friend like this. He was so much fun to be with and he always cracked him up with laughter. OC had a wonderful ability to know when to offer quiet support and advice. But today because of other engagements, OC had to be absent. Jonathan was very unhappy but theirs was that friendship that could never come close to shattering the bond.

It took Jonathan a long time to locate and contact OC on the cell phone. "Where in the world are you?" Jonathan asked with a desperate and curious voice.

"Jonathan, I hate this life, always on the road to have a deal with the executives in Europe for my dad. You know how it is! What's going on?" He was delighted to hear Jonathan's cheerful and ecstatic voice. "It seems like you are in high spirits."

Jonathan laughed for a minute. "Well, you won't believe what I am going to say. Pay attention. I am getting married in Hawaii to a Hawaiian girl. Her name is Oliana." For a moment there was a silence on the other side. "Are you still there, OC?" Jonathan asked in a restless voice.

"Yes, but I don't believe what you just said. But on the other hand, I am happy for you if it is true. Ah, a Hawaiian girl—she must be beautiful and sensual. I know that's the kind of girl you would be interested in. My only regret is that I won't be able to make it. I have to be here for few weeks. I wish I could get away to join you there but these appointments for the company were made earlier. I could not avoid it now. Anyway, congratulations and I will see you in Houston soon." His voice sounded sad.

Jonathan was very disappointed as well. He remembered how OC was always there for him as all best friends are. Jonathan had known OC for only three years, but they became best friends. After his 23rd birthday, Jonathan hung out with lots of friends from college, but OC was the one he liked the most. All of the other friends always wanted something in return except OC who had no hidden agenda or self interest. He remembered when they used to go to the car show or the boat show; he would always point out the one that had a good value even though money was not a concern. Jonathan remembered when OC used to beat him in swimming, he would not dwell on his victory instead he would say to Jonathan, "You are so good at tennis and not to mention all the other games. You always beat me, and I could never compete with you, and most of all I like your sincerity in everything." Jonathan felt overwhelmed with OC's comment about his generosity and would sincerely reply, "Well, I would rather have your intellectual ability, instead." OC would respond, "Oh, Ha! Ha! How about all the girls picking you over me – I wish I was that lucky." Both of them would start to laugh at this point. Jonathan could remember that vividly and though he wished OC was here, he could not dare think of postponing the marriage any longer. His brother Jason had not come either. That, of course, was expected for there was little love lost between them from childhood.

# Chapter 5

The executive jet, white and sleek, touched down and rolled to a stop on the runway almost alongside the black limo that had been parked there for the past half hour. Spencer Foster stepped out, squinting his eyes against the bright light of mid morning. Sophie, his wife, followed him down the steps and entered the limo.

"How could Jonathan do this to us?" she asked almost as soon as she had sat down.

"That's predictable. He wants to shock us; he always has."

"No. Not when he was a child. It was Jason who was so difficult as a child, not Jonathan. What came over him the last few years?"

They had been on a ship cruising in the Bahamas for the past couple of weeks and had had no contact with anyone. That was the way they wanted it, peace and quiet over the year-end, and the main reason they took the cruise. It was only when their ship had come into port that they had any news about their business or home. Even then they did not have an inkling of Jonathan's marriage, and it was only when their pilot handed them the mail that they knew what had happened. They could not believe it.

It was not something that they had expected. Of course they knew they would have little say in the women their sons chose as their wives. Sophie and Spencer had fallen in love with each other in a club and so would not have interfered with their sons on that issue. But it was not something that they had seriously considered, knowing full well that their sons would not allow any meddling in their lives. This, however, was something that they had not in their wildest imaginations thought would happen.

Spencer sat back and sighed. For a moment it seemed that he was going to sound forgiving. "I don't know, he works hard enough in the office and I can't complain about that. But his heart has not been in it, I know. It's impossible to fathom him."

"God knows why, but he doesn't seem to want to enjoy the good life," Sophie added.

"And he has the strangest friends. You've seen that Indian fellow he hangs around with. The one he calls OC, haven't you?"

"Half Indian, Spencer. I know his mother and I meet her quite often at the club. She is rather ok. She's a Stanhope."

"Yes, I do. I know his father. He's one of those Indians with all the trappings of success. He has a big BMW, a large house and is really very successful. In fact, I do some business with him. But the son, he's an oddball."

"I agree. But he's no problem, really."

"That's all very well, but what are we going to do about this Polynesian girl?" he asked exasperatedly.

"I wonder what she's like," Sophie mused aloud.

*In Pursuit of Love, Spirituality and Happiness*

"Oh, I can imagine - a gold digger. Pretty of course, but then they all are."

"We must not pre-judge. But I guess you're right."

"They've checked into the Hilton. That's a relief, Sophie. I wouldn't have wanted her to receive us at home."

"Yes," she agreed and then slumped into thought.

"But we'll have to throw a party," she said after a while.

"A party for them? Certainly not! We're not going to throw a party for Jonathan who disobeyed us."

"We'll have to. If we don't, their marriage will be the main topic of gossip for the next few weeks in every club and at every party in Houston. You know how it is! They need something to talk about and this will be the hottest news they can get their hands on. But if we throw a party, most of the gossip may die down."

"No!" he said emphatically as the limo turned and stopped before double gates made out of sheet metal and set in a 10-foot white wall. The main gate swung open of its own accord and they swept up the wide driveway that led to the front porch of their large two-storied white house with many windows. The mansion, built by Spencer's father more than 30 years ago, was a showpiece of modernism of the 50s, combining the futurism of that time with art deco and functionalism and it bore the genius outstanding ability of his father. A bit too much of it, Spencer had always felt. He often thought of renovating this mansion, but perhaps there were some things that were best left alone. His father's will had been specific about many things and some of it concerned the house and its preservation. Spencer did not want to risk losing it. Spencer walked through the foyer to the study that had been his father's, and now his, and seated himself behind the heavy desk. Sophie followed him.

"Spencer, don't you understand? We have to throw a party for them! We cannot afford to let Houston know that they got married without even telling us."

He looked at her then leaned back in his chair, built a pyramid with his hands and scowled at her over the peak of it and said, "I guess you're right, my dear. Well then, you talk to him."

"All right," she murmured.

"But will he agree? You know how he is."

"He will have to. He owes us that at least," she said determinedly

— — —

There was no escaping it; they had to meet Jonathan's parents. So, much against his gut feelings, Jonathan called them the day after Sophie and Spencer returned from their cruise, and told them that he and Oliana would be coming over. Later that day, a Sunday as it turned out, they went to the Foster mansion late in the afternoon. Oliana was impressed with the huge house. She knew that Jonathan was wealthy, but the huge opulent mansion with its décor of another age reeked of wealth of the kind that she had only seen in the movies and in the television shows about the rich and the famous. She wondered, not for the first time, what her reception would be like.

To her surprise Jonathan's mother received them in the foyer with a cheery smile.

"Hello Jonathan," she said as she embraced him.

"Hello," he said as he withdrew from the embrace. "Mother, this is Oliana."

Oliana looked at Jonathan's mother. Clearly she had once been a beauty. Her belly was still flat and although her waist had started to thicken a bit it was still youthful and her breasts seemed yet firm like that of a young woman. She looked far too young to be Jonathan's mother. Just went to show what Botox, collagen, and tuck in surgery could achieve—there were no creases at her mouth or eyes, at least they were not noticeable in the soft light in the foyer. And if there were, they could be held at bay a little longer with massages and cream. Sophie's hair, a mixture of amber and gold, gave credit to the abilities of her hairdresser. All in all, the package was very svelte, very slick and stylish.

Looking at her mother-in-law Oliana realized where her husband's good looks had come from. She suddenly felt a slight surge of affection for her. Why, she could not fathom at the time. Sophie surveyed her and then caught her by her shoulders and planted a perfunctory kiss on her cheek.

"Well, you must be tired, I will ask the maid to show you the lavatory where you can freshen up" she said as she drew back from the kiss. Oliana did not reply, and merely nodded her head. She needed some time to focus on her thought. Her momentary surge of affection was replaced by logic and sense. She knew instinctively that Jonathan's mother was in charge. The fact that she had not said a word of recrimination to Jonathan for his having married a Polynesian girl without even a word to them, revealed that. Oliana knew that she would have to be handled with care.

After Oliana came back, Sophie led the way to the drawing room where Spencer sat in a wing-backed chair. He did not smile and Oliana, having been set at ease by Sophie, was taken aback at the frosty stare he gave. He got up, nevertheless, and after being introduced allowed Oliana to give him a peck on his cheek and then returned to his seat and continued to idly turns the pages of the newspaper. Jonathan sat down beside her. Nobody said a word and Oliana wondered whether that was what they were like all the time or whether their unexpected and clearly objectionable wedding had occasioned it.

Just when she was almost at the end of her patience and wondering when someone would open up and talk, a young man entered the room. He was dressed in a designer white tennis shirt and expensive designer pants and carrying tennis racket in his hand. At first sight he looked like Jonathan's twin, but a closer look revealed eyes that were closer together, a mouth that was a lot wider, and a demeanor that was at once calculating and rascally. "Ah, there you are Jonathan! And this lovely girl must be the new bride, eh? What do I call you now, Jonathan? *Brah?*" he chortled, pleased with his own joke.

"I know a lot of Hawaiian jokes," he continued, looking at Oliana. Jonathan looked at his wife and then his eyes rose to the ceiling in exasperation. He knew what was coming and Oliana seeing his eyes staring at the ceiling had a good idea herself.

"What's the only suit a Hawaiian needs? A bathing suit!" This pronouncement too was followed by that grating cackling laughter. Was he trying to be friendly or was it deliberately mocking, Oliana wondered. Whatever his intentions, Oliana felt distressed.

"Oh shut up, Jason," Jonathan warned.

"Yes Jason, don't tease the poor thing," Sophie interjected, trying to diffuse the situation.

"It doesn't matter," Oliana said, although his attitude annoyed her more than she could say. Had it been on familiar territory she could have walked away.

"Mom, I'm only trying to be friendly. And she is really very good looking. Congratulations, brother. Don't worry I'm just leaving," Jason said, winking his eyes in Oliana's direction. There was no mistaking his keen attention to her.

"Jonathan, we would like to throw a party to welcome you both," Sophie began almost as soon as Jason had exited the room.

"No mother, I wouldn't like that."

"But you must! How can we face our friends if there's no party? They'll think that you married against our wishes. The truth is we did not even get a chance to make a protest. You owe us that at least."

"You know I hate crowds and also I have to know how Oliana feels about it," Jonathan protested.

"Yes, dear. But we won't call a large number. It will be a small one party, only our close friends."

He weighed that in his mind. There was no getting away from it he knew. "Well mother, if you must, but only cocktails," he said resignedly.

*In Pursuit of Love, Spirituality and Happiness*

They sat there for a while Oliana fidgeting and Jonathan trying to get a conversation going. Finally he stood up and catching Oliana by the hand announced, "We had better be going."

When they had left Sophie turned around and asked Spencer, "What are your impressions?"

"She's very good looking. That's an asset in a bride, whatever you may say about it."

"I don't say anything about it, Spencer. I know," Sophie murmured.

"She must be intelligent too. She said something about wanting to attend college."

"I guess it's not so bad after all. One look at her beauty and no one in Houston is going to have anything to say about us."

— — —

But cocktails it was not. Very small glasses of Dom Perignon in the drawing room with opened Colchester oysters and limes cut into quarter-moons laid out in beds of crushed ice. The men were elegant in their tuxedos and the women were dressed in the creations of the likes of Balenciaga, Givenchy, and Dior. The buzz of conversation, not all of it polite, filled the room as Oliana made her entry into the ballroom. Jonathan held her hand and gave her a wry smile. She found his warm firm clasp reassuring. Her tall, slim figure was clothed in fluted ivory silk, a Marcus Neiman gown, cut full enough to float on the air around her when she moved. Sophie had personally selected it. Around her neck was Jonathan's gift, given to her a day after they had landed in Houston - a choker with a diamond of some significance set in white gold that nestled in the hollow formed by her collar bones. Large diamond earrings glistened at her ears. They added just the right note, and she knew that she looked gorgeous and beautiful. Jonathan's impeccable evening clothes set off his classic good looks. They made a very spectacular couple, and she knew it. Her fingers, long and tapered, squeezed Jonathan's hand and reassured by the slight pressure of acknowledgement, continued to rest there.

"You look more beautiful than ever," Jonathan whispered in her ear.

"Don't make me more nervous than I already am," she whispered back.

"I love you."

Applause, a polite whispering of palms against palms, led by Sophie spread through almost the whole crowd, rose then sustained itself for a moment or two, then fell away. As if she was royalty, Oliana thought, as she felt all eyes on her. But then in another world, not this, she would have been. Jonathan stood by her side introducing her to the new world into which she would have to now make her new life.

The women were beautiful or had worked their beauticians to make them so. The jewelry on their hands and ears and around their necks would have graced the display windows of any of the top jewelers in the country. It was, after all, a gathering of the very chic and the very rich in the biggest city of a state that was well known for its wealth.

Never having been to a single high society party, Oliana had been apprehensive about it. It was even more daunting because she would be the cynosure of all eyes for whichever manner any guest viewed the situation. She would be either the exotic flower from the islands or the chirpy that the Foster boy brought home. And then there was the etiquette to be observed. Jonathan, however, told her not to worry on that score.

"It's a cocktail party, not a sit-down dinner. That's why I agreed to the party. So there's nothing to worry about. It's only caviar that you have to be careful about. It is unlikely that it will be served because most of the guests will be standing. If it is served, it is likely to be passed to you in a bowl with a spoon. In which case, serve a teaspoon onto your plate. When the accompaniments arrive, use the spoon provided and serve a few lemon slices and a couple of toast points. Then you just assemble a canapé to your taste with a knife and then use your fingers to put it in your mouth," he advised her. "And if you don't like to eat you don't have to. Don't worry; I will always be with you. I won't leave you alone," Jonathan assured.

Fortified by his advice, Oliana was able to view the party more objectively. After a while she felt a sense of detachment, as if she were on the outside looking in. It was strange, and she felt as though she was peering into a bowl of goldfish and that she could actually hear the fish talk.

White-coated waiters circulated through the crowd offering champagne and little platters of caviar and pate. There were cold cuts, including cold lobster, on the table in the room just beyond the ballroom. Oliana particularly liked the elegant, magnificent, white, sculptured swans made with the ice in every corner of the room and so many kinds of flower bouquets. Oliana did not even know the names. A photographer snapped a couple of shots of them looking lovingly at each other. Jonathan slipped an arm around her waist, and she felt comfortable and benign.

As the party progressed, the room gradually became crowded and the world outside seemed to become quieter as the babble within rose perceptibly. The conversation around her began to get cattier than she had ever heard. Big city gossip. She had no difficulty understanding every word of it, although she had not heard it before.

*"Her face lift is so taut that she gets lipstick in her earrings!"* One of the women said about another person who was not present in that party.

*"She looks like she was poured into that gown and forgot to say when."*

Then of course there were the men talking shop. She understood some of it.

*"Heck, John, you could have given me a tip on that one. Do you know how much I dropped last week?"*

*"But I had no idea. You know I'd have told you if I had."*

Not all the talk was as warm as that one. Some was as cold as the champagne that prompted them.

*"For the record I'll say it again. You are out of your mind."*

Then there were the ones who tried to talk to her, but finding no common ground were reduced to asking questions about Hawaii - questions to which Oliana was certain, they knew the answers. One matron in a dark blue dress rolled up to her side and asked, "Is it true, dear, that you Hawaiians call every one older than you Auntie or Uncle?"

It was on the tip of her tongue to say 'Yes, Auntie'. But she bit back that retort, nodded her head and smiled sweetly. Another guest, a man this time, wanted to know what *bumbye* was. She replied that it just meant "otherwise." The man smiled an odd smile and after waiting by her side for just another couple of minutes, moved away. Jonathan came to her side and asked, "Are you ok? Do not worry. I am always with you." Then he introduced OC. "Look who is here."

OC said, "Congratulations. I am sorry I could not make it at your wedding; you must have heard from Jonathan the reason why I could not make it. Anyway, I know you made Jonathan very happy."

This was the first time Oliana saw OC. She was impressed, and with every remark OC made, she felt even more enthusiastic and interested. Quietly, she was praising Jonathan's right choice of this friend. Then Jason came to her side, touched her shoulder, and planted a brotherly kiss on her cheek.

"You look fantastic. I wish I had made that trip to Hawaii," he whispered in her ear. She lifted one eyebrow and then smiled at the obvious flattery and flirtatious comment.

"Well you could still go there," pretending not to take any notice of the hint.

"But then you wouldn't be there," he smiled.

Have you been to Hawaii?" Oliana wanted to change the topic.

"No," he admitted.

"Well then you should. It's a beautiful place."

"I will if the girls are all like you."

"Why didn't you come for our wedding?" She again tried to change the subject.

The man was a Casanova and like all accomplished rakes was a charmer. Before she could think of a response to that Jonathan came to her side again and glancing at his sibling, steered her away.

Oliana was relieved. It was getting to be difficult trying to stave off his innuendoes. She did not want to say anything that would be misunderstood. Well, that took care of the brother. Sophie had played the doting mother-in-law's role to perfection. She had bought outfits from Saks, Marcus Neiman and the other top designers for Oliana. Was it because she had no role in the selection of her trousseau, Oliana wondered? But whatever it was she was pleased at the attention Sophie had given her and the gifts she had showered on her.

What surprised her most was Spencer. He no longer behaved as indifferently as he had on their first meeting. In fact he seemed to be pleased of the bride his elder son had brought home. Throughout the evening he introduced her to various guests and played the role of an accomplished father-in-law to the hilt. She wondered whether it was an act. It could be. He had been so cold and distant when they had first met and although that had thawed on their later meetings, he had not exhibited anywhere near the bonhomie that he exhibited throughout the party. That perhaps made it well worth the anxiety she had undergone and the scrutiny that she had to endure all evening.

# Chapter 6

Oliana, who had never ever been to mainland America, was awe struck by Texas in general and Houston in particular. Everything about the Lone Star state and its largest city was big. The state was the biggest state in the country after the bleak and almost barren Alaska. It was the nation's largest producer of petroleum and beef. Its state capitol was the biggest in the country. At 570 feet, the obelisk in the San Jacinto Battleground State historic park in Houston was the world's tallest obelisk and the Harris County Domed stadium was the world's first plastic-domed and air-conditioned sports arena. There were many other such impressive facts. It was not difficult to imagine that Texas was once an independent country.

Although she had well over the required grade point average of 3.0 on all graduate work at the University of Hawaii, which she would get credit for, she was told that the University of Houston required her to have in all 30 credit hours of which 24 had to be completed at that university itself. This meant that she would get credit for only two terms and would have to do the remaining terms. Overall, it meant the loss of a year. At first she was upset, but then Jason put things in a different perspective.

"You are not going to make a career of it, are you?" he teased, and continued. "Then what does it matter? As she objected to that conversation, Jonathan came to rescue. "You will learn a lot more. After all, it is yet another university with different professors and courses. You will get used to student life here in Houston, which I am sure will be very different from Hawaii. It will also give you knowledge and good experiences, don't you agree?"

She agreed as there was no objection to be made. Since it was only early January, she was well in time to make the necessary applications, but she had to wait a couple of weeks until her classes began.

– – –

Jonathan decided that since they had not really been on a honeymoon, they could do so before her college term started. He wanted her to choose, but she, having never been out of Hawaii before, left it to Jonathan to decide.

"Then I think we could go to Las Vegas. It's very glitzy and all that but it's so different from the resorts that most people go in their honeymoon. You know what it's like. Most resorts try to achieve the beauty and tranquility of Hawaii, but Las Vegas, on the other hand, is the very opposite. It's brash and perhaps even appears earthy to many. It's the very opposite of home."

Oliana was only too happy to agree to his suggestion as she only wanted to be with him wherever he wanted to go. Las Vegas was everything she had been told—a fun-loving city in the desert with sparkle and glitter 24 hours a day, a city of lights that proudly boasted that it never slept. They reached Las Vegas in the evening, and as they drove through the city to their hotel, past transplanted palms and instant shrubbery, Oliana stared at the casinos, the flashing neon signs, and the people who scurried all over the place bumping into each other. Oliana wondered what it was that prompted people to set up such a place in the middle of the desert and asked Jonathan.

"Till the 30s, Las Vegas was a forlorn railroad stop in the furnace desert. Then in 1931 the state of Nevada legalized gambling and within one month the city issued six gambling licenses."

"Six gambling licenses in a month!"

"Just imagine!"

"And then the Hoover Dam, America's largest dam, was built across the Colorado River, resulting in an influx of construction workers. And then Bugsy Siegel opened the Flamingo."

"Bugsy Siegel? Who was he?" she asked.

"He was a mobster from the east. He got gunned down in 1946."

"His luck ran out, I guess."

"Where else will it, obviously in Las Vegas!" Jonathan responded philosophically.

--- 

The hotel that Jonathan selected was literally out of this world. Their two-bedroom villa, one of 10 such, had its private garden with chaise lounges, outdoor tables set around a pool. At the end of the garden was a rock-rimmed pool in which goldfish cruised lazily. It had a king-sized round bed from which they could gaze at themselves through the huge mirror on the ceiling. Everything about the place was opulent, with Italian white marble and gold. It had a personal butler and private limousine service. There were "His" and "Her" bathrooms with Jacuzzi and steam baths, and hanging in the bathrooms of Italian marble and French onyx were Egyptian cotton towels, robes, and slippers. There were, and she counted them, nine telephones scattered through the villa.

Oliana wondered at the cost of it all, but by then she had good ideas about the glamorous life of the Fosters, and she knew that no matter what fancy amount Jonathan spent for the place, it would not make any difference in his wallet. They spent a week there reveling in the balmy weather, swimming daily in the hotel pool, and making love. In the evenings they went out to enjoy extravaganzas such as the Follies Bergere at the Tropicana Hotel and Hello Hollywood at the MGM Grand Hotel and of course the gambling, which was there in all its forms, catering to every whim and fancy of the high rollers. It was a dizzying kaleidoscope of sights and a stunning barrage to the senses.

"I'm told that these hotels spend hundreds of million dollars a year to attract big name talents each year."

"Hundreds of millions?"

"Yes. That's what I was told. That's one way of ensuring its claim to the title of Entertainment Capital of the world."

They made an arresting pair as they stood in the La Scena Lounge of the Venetian, the opulent hotel designed to look like the Doge's palace in Venice. Unselfconscious, absorbed in each other, they attracted a certain amount of attention even in Las Vegas where money and beauty seemed to compete for attention in equal measure. Now as they stood alongside the steady armies of slot machines and watched the buzz of activity in the casino, Jonathan said, "The best bet is to make a mind bet."

"A mind bet?"

"Yes honey, you stand behind the game, watch the action and attempt to predict the winner. You never bet real money, you bet only in your mind."

Understanding the humor in it she laughed mischievously and responded "But then in the process you could lose your mind."

'Jonathan made a face and then asked, "What has a whole bunch of little balls and screws old ladies?"

Oliana was a bit shocked at the question, but before she could ponder over it he laughed and said, "Slot machines! Got you there, didn't I?"

But then, what was the point of being in Las Vegas if one did not bet? So they bought chips and went from table to table, trying out the different games. They did not bet much but it was thrilling for her nonetheless to win a bit of money now and then. She finally came away with a few tokens, which she decided to keep as souvenirs to remind her of this magnificent memory of their honeymoon.

They went to Los Angeles, too. Oliana was enthralled by the place, particularly Hollywood. She loved everything from the sleazy Hollywood Boulevard with its star imprinted sidewalks to the palm-lined streets of Beverly Hills.

Surprisingly, it was the return flight on the corporate jet that had the Foster's logo emblazoned on its tail that was the most exciting part of their honeymoon. They exchanged a honeymoon kiss as soon as they were settled in their seats. The stewardess looked on and smiled and then retreated to the tiny galley after leaving a plate of caviar and an ice bucket complete with a bottle of champagne and two crystal flutes on the table.

Jonathan picked up the bottle looked at it. "Moet et Chandon," he murmured approvingly, "Want some champagne, my love?" he asked.

She said lovingly "yes" and then he lifted one of the flutes, poured the wine carefully into it, and handed it to her. When he had filled the other glass, he lifted it and said, "Here's to you my very exotic, beautiful flower."

Oliana kissed him all over and then started to laugh softly but contentedly. "I don't want the caviar you know."

Jonathan did not hear what she was saying, only looked at her with an amused smile and reflected on how wonderful it had been these last few weeks. He could see that they had developed a fondness for much of each other's way of life. Although they kept to their own views and perspectives, they were able to filter out the best of both worlds and make their life together quite their very own and happy.

Together they guzzled the wine and got sillier by the glass until the aircraft landed in Houston.

– – –

*In Pursuit of Love, Spirituality and Happiness*

Oliana had hoped that Jonathan would take an apartment, but to her chagrin they went straight from the airport to the beautiful mansion. "Are we going to live here, now?" she asked as the car swept into the huge stone driveway.

"Well we can't stay at the Hilton forever, can we?"

"I thought we would be moving into an apartment of our own," she replied plaintively as the car lurched to a stop in the wide driveway.

"Look at this place! It's huge and I know you will love it as you stay here. I want to share with you whatever I have. You deserve the best. This is our home and as I got used to it you will too in time. Does it matter all that much if we don't have an apartment of our own now, honey?"

Just then the huge sculptured electric doors opened and the servants and maids stepped out from the mansion and Oliana sat back with the words in her mouth. There was nothing she wanted to say. Her beautiful large eyes broadened with surprise realizing that this was something that Jonathan had wanted her to try and she did not want to hurt him by suggesting something else.

They entered the house, leaving the baggage in the car to be handled by the servants. Jonathan led her up the stairs to his suite of rooms on the second marble floor. It was lovely set of rooms, comprised of a huge bedroom with an attached bathroom that had a sunken tub, a bookshelf-lined study, and a wood-paneled living room, which seemed well appointed in terms of furniture, mostly antique, and was like the rest of the house full of artifacts. However, unlike other living rooms that she had seen, it was bereft of any modern equipment. She was to discover later that all the accoutrements of modern life—even a home theatre with surround sound—were there, but they were carefully recessed and concealed in the woodwork and came into view only when required with a touch of a button.

Although for a moment she felt a sense of isolation as she stood there and she could not fathom why, but she suddenly realized that it was not such a bad idea to stay in this mansion, like a dream come true. And though it would have been nice to have an apartment of her own, she could get used to this large and rambling house, with its treasures, statues, antiques, beautiful garden with a huge swimming pool, and little private lake with the swans, and of course the many servants that she had seen only in the movies.

Yes, she would. In her entire life she had never been attended by anyone, never loved so much by someone as Jonathan, and never had anything like all the fancy dresses and jewelry to make her even more beautiful.

---

She had a week left before the semester began and wondered what to do with her time. Jonathan was away at work for most of the day and when he returned, he was happy to spend time with her. She decided to put her free time to good use by going back to her old love of visiting museums and galleries, and Houston had many such institutions. Of course there was no question of going around on her own as the aristocratic and sophisticated people like Jonathan's would not permit that. The family had two limousines and at least one car and chauffeur would be around all the time. Sophie insisted that Oliana should not go anywhere except in one of these cars. So she used the limousines and went around town. That took care of quite a bit of her time and although she was not fully occupied, she was happy and content.

She loved her bedroom even more. There was something warm and friendly about it, and she discovered a sense of tranquility that she had never found before. Was it because it had been Jonathan's for so long, a bed in which no one but he had slept before? Most days she would stir awake in the huge round silk-sheeted bed, slowly becoming aware that she was alone and that the light that filtered past the half-opened shutters, through lacy curtains, still held the gentleness of dawn. Jonathan would be out on his daily morning run, but invariably, by the time she got up see Jonathan's smiling face, Jonathan could not wait to make love with her again.

After a morning spent in an art gallery or museum it was good to be back home in the bedroom. It was nice to be back in the comfort of their suite, in the huge mahogany bed with the cream bedspread. Was it the room or was it her happiness of life with Jonathan? She did not want to dwell for long on such philosophical questions.

As the days went by, she began to actually like the house. There were surprises at practically every corner. Sophie, she was later to learn, had had feelings similar to hers when she entered the house as a young bride. It was she who had added the touches that made it such an interesting place. Over the years, she had changed the décor, bought exquisite pieces of art and expensive artifacts and transformed the house from a somber place to a bright, exquisite, impressive one.

Oliana also enjoyed going down to the little lake and feeding breadcrumbs to the milk-white swans that glided over its waters. Surely it was a dream, she told herself. One of these days she would wake up and find that it was all gone.

— — —

Her first day at college was quite different from her first day at university in Hawaii. She did not experience quite the rush she had then, when she had been apprehensive about the work she had to do and worried about how she would fare. Here, it was the social element that was daunting. Even though there were students from all over the world, she stood out. That was something she was learning to cope with day by day. Yet everything seemed strange and new. She knew that these feelings would disappear in time once she was into the rhythm of the place.

But she did not have to fit into anyone's pattern and soon began to gain confidence in herself. She started to take note of all that was going on around her in the class, and, in time, came to the realization that people did not want to be understood completely. If they did, perhaps they would have nothing left. She couldn't quite figure it out, but she got the feeling that most of the time they just wanted to be taken for granted. A bit carelessly, she thought.

It was a new strange feeling of touching many people superficially, yet without being touched herself. Once college started, her routine changed. She woke up at the same time she had woken before, but thereafter the tempo changed for she had to be ready to get to college on time.

Invariably they went sailing on the weekends. An outdoor man himself, Jonathan introduced her to a lot of activity like sailing and hang-gliding. He had a yacht, the *Kestrel*, a 42-foot Jeannean Sun Odyssey with a fiberglass hull and two cabins, one aft and the other forward. It was blue and white and although essentially a sailing craft, had a single diesel engine. On most Saturdays and Sundays, they would pack provisions and go sailing. They would drive down to where the *Kestrel* had been moored and sail down to Galveston Bay, an inlet of the Gulf of Mexico. Oliana found it most enjoyable and soon became a good sailor. She preferred that to hang-gliding. Jonathan would often tell her, "Sailing is in your genes, my love."

But the weekends when Jonathan was not around, Sophie wanted Oliana to be involved with several of her charitable organizations. She was always attending one meeting or the other at Sophie's request. Sometimes she would have the meeting in the house and if Oliana were home she would be asked to join in. She couldn't possibly refuse. After all, it was for charity. Soon, however, she began to take pleasure in high society life. She had never been used to luxury and the opulence that she saw in the Foster home and in the homes of their friends. It soon swept her off her feet. It was such a far cry from her small home in Hawaii.

Sophie took her shopping almost every week. They invariably went to the shops that sold the most expensive of clothes and jewelry and sometimes Sophie even picked out Oliana's clothing for her. It upset Oliana initially, but then she realized that Sophie had exquisite taste and that whatever clothing and accoutrements she chose for her always suited her to perfection. So she fell in with practically everything Sophie suggested. It was a bit difficult at first because most Hawaiians went for bright and colorful clothing, whereas in mainland America the top designers were far more subdued. Over time, she acquired a taste for the right kind of clothing to please Sophie.

Sophie began taking her to the clubs that they were members of and introduced her to her circle of friends. They were all well-heeled and moved around in the same social circles. Most of them had little to do other than go to the clubs or to afternoon soirees, attend fashion shows, art exhibitions, and dabble in charity. Sophie's exotic daughter-in-law was at first a curiosity, but soon her sweet nature won them over and she became a great hit with them.

But there were the usual gaffes. After the first few outings Sophie began to hint as to what Oliana ought to say in polite company. She knew how important the knowledge of courtesy and good manners were in the company she moved around in, and when she found that it was not having the desired result, Sophie quietly recruited Jonathan to her cause. It was difficult for Oliana to heed Sophie's every instruction, but when it was Jonathan who made the suggestion, she had no problem and never had to be reminded again. Soon, like her grace and beauty, it came naturally to her.

– – –

Oliana made a few friends at the university and Jonathan, tired though he would be after work, was happy and contented. After objecting on the day of their return from their honeymoon about staying in the mansion, Oliana made no further attempt to Jonathan to move out. She realized that although Jonathan did not have an easy relationship with his father, he doted on his mother. She also realized that Jonathan had seen in her a person who would complement well into his household. Once she realized that, Oliana gave up any lingering thoughts of moving out and decided to make the best of what she had. After all, they had a large suite all to themselves and if they wanted to get away they could always go on board the *Kestrel*. Once she gave up on this quest, life seemed to pass by quickly and smoothly.

– – –

Her friend Susan Collins was such a comfort. Oliana had gotten to know her in college in Houston and liked her almost from their very first meeting. Susan was, unlike most girls, very down to earth and carefree and she seemed to know everything. In her attitudes and manner of speaking, she reminded Oliana of what she read in books about children of the 60s, the ones who advocated peace and free love and were anti establishment. She was great fun to be with and Oliana, recognizing in her a kindred spirit spent a lot of her free time with her.

When Jonathan began working longer hours or when he was away on business trips, she was happy that she had Susan for company. It was to her that Oliana poured out her heart. Although Jonathan was most devoted to her and attentive to all her needs, she could not quite express everything at the same level. And also he did not have any time for a long conversation. Susan seemed to empathize with Oliana. They would talk hours about politics, love, customs, and sometimes, Oliana's family. Susan was studying law. Though she was much older than Oliana, the amiable spirit in her was fascinated by this beautiful, different, and simple Hawaiian girl.

One Monday afternoon when Susan was crossing the path leading to the huge, quiet library, she saw Oliana reading a book in the reference library. She did not waste any time and stopped in front of her. "Hi there," she said in a cheery smile.

"I am so bored with studying today" Oliana said.

"Why don't we go out and take some fresh air," Susan suggested.

"Great idea, let's go."

Susan did not expect Oliana to leave studying and go with her so quickly. They sat down on the well-maintained plush green lawn where lots of other students were gossiping, studying, laughing, and even kissing. This was the fourth time she had spent time with Susan.

"I am sorry if I have to ask you a personal question—it bothered me a great deal to ask. Susan, why didn't you ever get married," Oliana was puzzled.

"That's a long story," Susan answered.

"Oh, but I really want to know. I don't have any more classes today. I have plenty of time to listen."

*In Pursuit of Love, Spirituality and Happiness*

"Are you sure?" Susan was hesitating.

"I really ought to know you better. Tell me about you."

At Oliana's persistent requests Susan started. "I know you have no idea about 1968. That was the time when so many things happened. I was 19 years old and studying at Columbia University. The country was in a charged mood—chaos everywhere. The conservatives were overtaken by a full-blown social and political revolt, even in Paris. The civil rights movements broke out.

Then in April, Dr. Martin Luther King was assassinated. There were so many political demonstrations about the Vietnam War and disapproval of President Johnson's handling of the war. We took over Columbia University's administrative building, and eight days later police were called in and we were arrested. My boy friend, Anthony, was arrested as well and was beaten. He was in charge of that demonstration. Finally, we were released but Anthony was in great pain. He started taking narcotics long before the time of the flower or hippie movement. He was addicted to narcotics. I tried many ways to help him, but it was too late. I loved him so much and still do even after his death. It has been a long time." She paused for a while. Oliana did not say anything but her eyes full of tears dripping down to her cheeks said everything. Afterwards, they both left for home.

The next morning, Susan invited Oliana to have a cup of coffee with her. Susan did not waste any opportunity to ask Oliana about her customs and history of her country as she was planning to visit Hawaii again with a different perspective. As she was learning from Oliana - her passion for the Hawaiian island infused with local mythologies –vibrant and lively Susan was thinking she would go to Hawaii again and have a different cultural experience.

"I hope you don't mind if I ask you about the real history of Hawaii, your homeland. When I visited before, all I did was surf, go to see the commercial hula dancing show, and eat luau on the table sitting on a bench. Of course, I would not dispute Mark Twain who referred to Hawaii as the loveliest fleet of island that has anchored in the sea. But until now, I didn't know anything about the early history of Hawaii. Please tell me about that."

Overwhelmed by Susan's enthusiasm, Oliana took a deep breath and said, "I hope you won't be bored with my telling the history of Hawaii."

"Of course, not." Susan was desperate to know.

Oliana started again with a pause "Until the fifth or sixth century, the Hawaiian Archipelago was no man's land—an inhabited paradise. My mom said that the Europeans visited Hawaii as early as the 16th century, but the British party of Captain James Cook landed on Kauai in January 1778. He named the Archipelago the Sandwich Islands, in honor of the fourth earl of Sandwich, then head of the British Admiralty."

"Really?"

"Kamehameha I gained control of the island in a 10-year war and by 1795 he held all the main islands except Kauai and Nihau, which he added in 1810. Later, an American missionary, William Richards, became a government advisor, and not long afterward the first constitution was written."

"Is it like our government in U.S.?"

"Yes, the government of Hawaii has legislative, executive, and judicial branches. The personal and property rights which we call Great Mahele, the division of lands, were created. That was the greatest achievement. In 1842, the U.S. indirectly recognized the independence of Hawaii, and Gerrit P. Judd, an American missionary, served the kingdom as prime minister. At the same time, Hawaii was becoming a major supply base for American whaling ships. In 1875, during the reign of Kalakaua, Hawaiian signed a treatise with the U.S. permitting easy access to American markets for Hawaiian sugarcane. Later, Queen Liliuokalani was deposed in 1893, and Sanford B. Dole, a Hawaiian-born American, headed the republic of Hawaii. Two years later, on June 14, 1900, Hawaii was constituted a U.S. territory and Dole became the first governor. The U.S. entered World War II after a surprise Japanese assault on Pearl Harbor and airfields on Oahu. In the post- war period, my ancestors enjoyed economic growth, spurred in large part by tourism and military spending."

Susan was impressed with Oliana's detailed knowledge, and then she remembered Oliana was majoring in Hawaiian history. "Interesting, what happened then? She asked with curiosity.

"Sadly in late 40s and 50s, there were considerable numbers of labor strikes by sugarcane and pineapple workers. Our country had a lot of difficulty – unemployment was high. Now tourism is the leading industry in Hawaii."

Susan was delighted and said "Yes, Hawaiians are friendly people, their smile welcomes the stranger. I like that—especially when they say 'Aloha' to everybody. That implies love and peace, and you are no exception." Susan's remark made Oliana happy.

She commented, "I am also glad that Hawaii became a state. Our people are very grateful for tourism from the mainland—without that we would not be able to make it, especially my parents."

Oliana was so engaged with the conversation she did not realize it was getting late. Soon she had to leave for classes.

– – –

The next day when they were returning from school, Oliana talked to Susan again to find out what Susan thought about the hula. She pursued her with questions about the dance.

"Do you think hula dance was erotic?" Oliana asked Susan.

"I can imagine that lot of people think that way!"

"I know the hula dance today is no longer what it formerly was in the tradition of the Hawaii. What you see today is taught for commercial purposes to please the eyes of people, for tourist attraction—this degeneration made me sad. But I am talking about long time ago, that ancient, possessed feelings when the dance was dedicated to the Goddess Pele originally, it was spiritualist and mystical—that feeling, that essence."

Though Susan knew how the Hawaiian people feel about Hula dance, she said in a doubtful voice "But does the hula dance really represent your people?"

"Hula, to the outside world, is just an erotic dance. But to the Hawaiian it is a living art form that represents life. It is an integral part of our culture," Oliana said in a mystic voice.

"Isn't there anything else that represents Hawaiian culture?"

"Well nothing exemplifies it as much as hula does. Susan, you have to understand that hula is not the simple dance by nubile Hawaiian girls that you may have seen in movies like Blue Hawaii. Women performed the hula, of course. But most of the performers in the old days were men. The real hula is very symbolic and its gestures portray hidden meanings. Hula expresses everything that we see, feel, hear, smell, taste, and touch, and the chants celebrate procreation and, naturally, sex. These are what makes hula both powerful and stimulating."

"I guess we know only what we see on television or in the movies."

"Hula is the history book of our people," Oliana continued.

"History?" Susan asked, arching an eyebrow.

"Yes. We Hawaiians had no written language till the missionaries came. For more than 1,000 years our traditions and history were kept alive through the chants that accompanied the hula dance."

Susan wanted to know about the origin of the hula dance and asked, "Do you know how hula originated?"

"Of course, I know the tradition."

"And what is that?"

"Hula is believed to have originated when the goddess Hiiaka danced to appease Pele."

"Pele, the Brazilian soccer player?" Susan asked with a giggle.

"Soccer player?" she asked in surprise. Then, realizing that she was just kidding, said, "Pele, the goddess of volcanic fire and Hiiaka's sister."

"Why did she have to be appeased?"

"That is a long story. When Pele is sleeping, the Hawaiian Islands are quiet, but when the goddess awakens, the earth roars and lava explodes from the mountains. Her spirit still inhabits the volcanoes."

"But what has that got to do with the hula dance?" Susan asked.

"When Pele wakes up from her slumber, she is at her most destructive. Then only hula will propitiate her."

"Surely you don't believe that, Oliana!"

"Well, I have been reading a great deal about dances from all over the world. Lots of communities the world over, dance to bring on the rains and many religions believe in the power of the dance."

"That's true."

"The Hindus, I have read, have a God called Shiva. Shiva is also known as the Lord of the Dance and Nataraj, the icon of that form of Shiva, is said to represent the essence of Indian heritage. Nataraj's cosmic dance typifies the eternal rhythm, the perfect balance between life and death."

"But not Christianity!" Susan exclaimed.

Susan just could not imagine the priests of the Catholic Church swaying to any form of dance.

"Christianity too. If you look in the Bible you will find a verse in the Psalms that says Let them praise His name in the dance. I am sure that there must be other similar verses, after all most of the psalms were composed by King David and I remember learning in Sunday school that King David used to dance to honor God. Perhaps it is only fitting that the hula should have been revived by another King David."

Susan, the flower child of the new century, had little knowledge of the religion she was born into other than what was chanted in the

Catholic church. She merely shrugged her shoulders and said, "Oh, I didn't know that."

"The point is that the ancient Hawaiians worshipped the one Creator God through their dance the hula."

"But we don't dance in church," Susan protested.

"You may not, but the blacks do. Don't they? There is nothing wrong in dancing. Man has always danced for many things—to please God, to please kings and queens, to bring rain and to woo the opposite sex. It is inherent in us and in most animals. Some of us may have been conditioned to suppress our feelings and so will not dance spontaneously, but it is there within us waiting to explode into action."

"I guess you're right."

Seeing Oliana's inquisitions in dancing Susan suggested that she should take some dancing lessons as a credit course.

"It is too late," Oliana said.

"It's never too late. Of course you will never become a professional dancer when you start so late, but the classes may help you to understand forms of dance other than your own and that will help."

Oliana mulled over that for a while and then decided that there was nothing much to lose and perhaps a lot to gain. It taught the rudiments of modern American dance, if nothing else. It would give her the exercise she needed to practice her dancing. And it did indeed, but she also learned a great deal about dance in general.

It was perhaps the happiest period in her life. She had a loving and devoted husband, she had a lovely magnificent home, she was attending a good university and studying the subjects of her choice, she had a close friend to whom she could open up without any inhibition and most of all, there were no monetary problems.

For that moment, she thought of her mother who would be the happiest-she knew that. But would this lovely spell last, she asked herself.

# Chapter 7

By the second year, towards the end of her university course, Oliana began to feel disenchanted with life in Houston. It was a good life, but the magic of the honeymoon was fading and although they still went sailing, it was not as often as in the early days after their marriage. On some weekends, Jonathan would take her to musical and theatrical productions or to the symphony and when there were no new productions, he would take her to museums where there were special shows on a variety of subjects.

However, Jonathan was becoming increasingly busy in his job and his mind was occupied with many things regarding the company's financial affairs. Oliana sensed that Jonathan was over-absorbed with his thoughts. Oliana could not figure it out and she did not know how to confront him in this situation.

At the breakfast table, as usual, he would always give Sophie a hug and a kiss on her cheek, making it plain for all to see how fond he was of her. His mother also devoted herself to giving lots of love to Jonathan when she not busy with her outside activities and defended him from any pain or hurt. Then Jonathan would kiss Oliana and hold Oliana's hand and sit by her side and look at her in a way that would say that she was the best thing to happen to him.

Sophie was very effusive and went out of her way to be friendly with Oliana, but Oliana often thought that she had no freedom in anything, no choice for her own dress, jewelry. Often she was instructed by Sophie what she had to say in front of her friends and acquaintances in her charity club. After attending a few of Sophie's charities, Oliana realized that it was not for her. Oliana's mind was not in it. The way Sophie was devoted to her charity and looked so glamorous and beautiful, and her contribution made such headway - it reminded Oliana of late princess Diana. But Oliana was different. Her mind would only get joys from the mystic volcano, the sumptuous river, the far away mountains, and loving Jonathan but not from artificial glamour. Spencer, although he was courteous and outwardly friendly, often struck her with the thought that he was using her at his advantage to acquire more deals for his company too. He would occasionally say to Oliana "you are an asset, my dear." Oliana knew exactly what he meant by this. All those thoughts about not joining with Sophie's charity and Spencer's attitude towards her were bothering her a great deal. But she was astute enough not to mention this thought to Jonathan as she saw how fond Jonathan was for his family.

Of course, Jason she saw very little because he was out of town a lot and although he had his set of rooms in the Foster mansion, he had a bachelor pad in town where he entertained his bevy of nubile young women and consumed large amounts of alcohol and drugs. She came to know about this from Jonathan. Jason was athletic and in his high school days had played football and baseball and taken part in track and field events with both great gusto and a fair amount of success.

Although now he spent a lot of time on the tennis courts and in the gym and caring for his racing car, Oliana never ever saw him at home much. Their timing never coincided. The one thing Jonathan seemed to have in common with his brother was his love of sailing. Like his brother, Jason too had a boat. She had not seen it, but Jonathan had told her that it was bigger and even more luxurious than the Kestrel.

Although Jason paid very little attention to work and went to the office only once or twice a week, he was there at all the parties that his parents threw. That was where Oliana and he came face to face. On these occasions, he always focused his attention on her and was at his charming best. She knew that she was being observed and admired by his thirsty eyes. Most of the times he was irreverent and would invariably sidle up to her when she was standing alone somewhere in the ballroom of the mansion and whisper, "You look stunning as usual."

She did not respond to any of his overtures but he remained courteous and outwardly friendly and often tried to lighten the mood. But it did not make her feel better or even any different; it only made her feel uncomfortable in his presence. She could not put her finger on it, but she could sense an underlying current of wickedness in her brother-in-law.

Jason, for his part, was infatuated with his new sister-in-law. She was at once the most accessible, yet the most distant. Had his relations with Jonathan been good, he could have perhaps had a good and healthy relationship with her. But it was impossible now. Oliana was such a lovely creature and oh so pliant in her ways. Jason usually had his way with the women who came into his life, but he had no idea of what Oliana thought of him. She was always friendly, but then that was the way she was with everyone. Every time he saw her the hunger grew because she was out of reach.

The Fosters, like all wealthy Texans, entertained quite a lot in their huge and luxurious mansion. As the hostess-in-waiting, Oliana had to suffer the attention of the phalanxes of tuxedoed Texans that were always there. The Fosters surrounded themselves with men of wealth—the most brilliant lawyers, the most distinguished physicians, enormously wealthy bankers, senators and even the governor.

Although the house, with its beautiful garden and wealth of antiques and artifacts that were strewn around it and the guests no longer awed her, Oliana now felt out of place in the Foster mansion. Oliana did notice that emotion did not hold any real value for Spencer. Spencer always wanted to acquire his status and his power in the society and he did not care how he achieved it.

Sophie was kind of person who loved to show her enormous wealth, and did not care what Van Gogh had painted or in what color or what subject matter was projected, but she was proud of owning the painting that had brought the praise and the status and the power in her society. Sophie had craved that all the time. The exception was Jonathan. He was an oasis for Oliana. Oliana had never dealt with the dark side of life. So in spite of being full of people and the bright lights that blazed throughout the mansion on a party night, it was now become cold and empty.

At one such party she found the atmosphere stifling. She looked around for Jonathan and, not spotting him anywhere, went upstairs to their suite to give herself some rest from the crowd. There she entered the bathroom and spent some time looking at herself in the mirror. When she re-entered the bedroom, however, she found it in darkness. She was sure that she had not switched off the light before entering the bathroom and groped for the switch in the darkness.

Suddenly the room was bathed in light and she felt herself being held by strong hands that went around her waist. She felt their rough warmth through the silk of her dress and looked up. His eyes looking intensely glinting into hers were worldly and knowing, and somehow wicked. She twisted away from him.

"What are you trying to do?" she asked, in fear and anger.

"Come on. You can't deny that you are attracted to me," he whispered in that gravelly teasing voice that had so irritated her on their first meeting.

"Please get away from me!" she pleaded, "Get away from me!" she exclaimed, outraged yet afraid to make too much noise.

His wide mouth smiled and his taunting eyes took in her full length. As she tried to dodge past him, he caught her and drew her gasping and struggling and helpless against his lean, muscular body. Oliana, fighting single mindedly to be free of him, was only vaguely aware of the presence of another. There was a sudden thud and then she was suddenly released and Jason was down on the ground. Oliana stared helpless and open mouthed as he scrambled to his feet, his hand going to his jaw where he had evidently been struck.

Oliana turned on her rescuer. It was Jonathan, grim faced and narrow eyed. Oliana collapsed on Jonathan's hand and closed her eyes in fear. She did not want to wake up from the bad dream. She could hear Jonathan's voice echoed in the air "you ought to be ashamed of yourself, shame on you." Jonathan knew Jason had been drinking.

– – –

Yet, the Foster parties were events she could not stay away from, except occasionally, and then only on the pretext of some illness. She could, however, avoid the ones they were invited to. Jonathan, too, did not like going to most of them and she knew which hosts he did not particularly like and would suggest crying out of the ones that were thrown by such people. So there was rarely an issue. But she was to most of the guests yet an anachronism, a curiosity and to some a source of amusement. At home life had begun to drift into a pattern.

"How was your day?" Jonathan would invariably ask on his return from work at late night.

"Not bad," was her standard reply.

He would then stand behind her and say, "Not good, either, huh?" as his arms went round her. Oliana was happy at his thoughtfulness but was sickened by all the superficial aggravation of life as offered in Houston. Hawaii and the fun- filled life of courtship in the early months before marriage was missing and she often wondered. She began thinking more and more about her home in Hawaii. In the privacy of their lovely suite of rooms, she would think about her dreams and about her life on Hawaii. Every now and then, her thoughts would drift to the dance of the islands and the powerful rhythm of the sharkskin drums, the split bamboo rattles, the bamboo stamping tubes, and the castanets made of stone would fill her ears - freedom to do anything, to go anywhere, swimming in any pond and the Hilo's charming mountain lava. When this happened she would almost unconsciously extend her arms out in front keeping her hands flat at waist level and push down with her fingers and then up and down again.

She would only be vaguely aware that she was acting out the hula gesture for moana, the ocean. Was it the ocean that she missed so much? She realized that her world was increasingly becoming alien. Susan, knowing what was happening began to don the mantle of protector. She was always around and though Jonathan did not take to her as warmly as Oliana had, he was nevertheless friendly with her and was pleased that Oliana had found a good friend. Susan seemed to have a level head on her shoulders and nothing in their relationship caused him any worry.

But he would have been surprised if he could have read her thoughts or got even a glimpse of Oliana's feelings. For him, no one was quite like Oliana. No moment with her was ever boring or dull. In his eyes she was a bubbly creature always full of surprises, knowledge, intellect ideas, plans, all rushing up from that wellspring of her colorful, carefree, yet independent, nature. Almost from the beginning, he had a sense of extreme good fortune as if he, through some slot machine, had won a jackpot, a prize desired by others. And he could sense that others too desired Oliana. He could see it in their eyes when he introduced her to his friends and business acquaintances.

You can have everything that money can buy and still be bored to death. Perhaps that was the reason for the boredom. What was it someone had said? The desire for desires; yes that was what boredom was. Once your desires were sated, boredom had to set in. She had everything she could possibly want and perhaps even more than what she wanted, with Sophie showering her with expensive gifts.

"Your mother gives me so many presents."

"Yes, I noticed. She's very fond of you."

"But I can't even go shopping for myself."

"Are you not happy with that?"

"No, darling, I was merely expressing something I just thought of."

"Oh," he murmured and then said, "I think I know what you mean." But Oliana knew from his tone that her husband had no idea what she had meant. She would have been thrilled to know that Jonathan loved her just the same as always, perhaps even more. That she got on so well with everyone was perhaps the one factor that made all the difference. But Jonathan did not know how to make Oliana believe all that he felt as she needed that. Being away from her people and among strangers was not easy and it would have helped if Jonathan had been aware of that. Jonathan did have a hunch of all of that but if it meant losing Oliana, he did not want to face the thought.

--- 

It was the University of Houston that gave Oliana the only focus in her life now. But the problem was that the course was drawing to an end. She had nothing more to learn from the dance composition that she took as the credit course which was designed to teach students the compositional form of emphasizing dance movements and it was both creative and innovative in its approach, but it was not a free form of dancing what Oliana was craving. It was with apprehension that she viewed the fast approaching end of college. What would she do once all this was over? She wondered. Oliana could not see anything outside of college and that thought hounded her doggedly for she did not want to study any further and she could not take up a job. It was so absorbing that it loomed all out of proportion. She thought so much about it that she became discouraged. And when she was discouraged, she couldn't do anything.

Jonathan was wrapped up in work at the family's business headquarters in downtown Houston. But she knew that his heart was not in it. After all, he did not need the money. It was fine as long as she was busy studying, but with the end of the final term looming, it was going to be frustrating for her to be in the mansion all day and wait for Jonathan to come home late in the evening. She often asked him why he went there and worked so hard if he did not want to. After all he did not need the money.

"Father wants me to be there," he would mutter.

"But you say that he does not involve you in many of the issues."

"That may be so, but he is out of town such a lot these days. You know those Middle East deals. Someone has to hold the fort."

"He has enough people to help him."

"Yes, but they are not family."

Oliana rarely raised any issues about the business and involved herself only when Jonathan made any mention of it. So, as abruptly as she had embarked on the uncomfortable questions, Oliana changed the subject.

"Why don't you stay in this weekend?" she asked.

"Ok, my love," he replied.

"Well, what do you want for dinner?"

"You."

"Besides that."

"What else do I need, my love," he said as he rumpled her hair fondly. Then he suddenly struck his hand on his forehead and said, "Oh, there's the Hascomb's dinner on Saturday. I'd forgotten about it." The moment was gone. "Then we don't have to go," she murmured.

"No, we can't. Norman Hascomb is crucial to our new deal and we have to be there."

"Darling, I'm awfully tired."

"No you can't cry out of this one, Oliana!"

Oliana did not rise to the barb. She could never bring herself up to that. She lapsed into silence. The thought of having to go yet another formal party was daunting to say the least. There was never anyone there she could relate to. The women were all the same. They spent most of their time working hard at making themselves look beautiful.

And so were the settings - white wine chilling in silver buckets, snow-white table linens. The only things plastic there would be on the faces and in the smiles of the people. Jonathan could not be around her all the time and invariably she had to stand sipping slowly from a glass of wine and trying to fend off the attentions of a guest who had had one too many.

In any event, she did go to the Hascomb's party and heard the same conversation, the men talking stock and the women gossiping as always about their status, dresses, jewelry, botox, and Hollywood's latest trend and style.

Oliana suffered the boredom in silence and thought of Hawaii and the carefree abandon of her people and of how noisy and enjoyable a party on the islands would have been.

— — —

When the party was over, they drove home in silence, each busy with their own thoughts. When Oliana returned to the privacy of the bedroom in their suite, she felt a gentle sadness wash over her. Her face crumpled into tears, and she cried softly to herself, "Oh, God, I can't stand it anymore."

Jonathan entered the room and hearing the muffled sobs came quickly to her side.

"What is the matter, my love?" he asked.

"I can't take it anymore."

"Take what?"

"All of it," she wailed.

His voice began to crack and grow soft as he lowered his eyes. "Oliana, just listen to me. Don't worry so much. Everything will be alright, you will see."

As his voice broke and faded away, he realized that there were tears on her face. Then he went around and put his arms around her, wiping her tears and letting her rest her head on his broad shoulder. They stayed like that for hours until at last she fell asleep. He smoothed the covers around her and touched her cheek and kissed her cheek repeatedly ever so gently. She looked so young, very young, and so beautiful, he thought, as she slept with no trace of sadness on her face. The bitterness of what could happen to a life out in the big, bad, ugly world was no longer there.

# Chapter 8

The headquarters of Foster Holdings Incorporated occupied six floors of glass and aluminum skyscraper in downtown Houston. There were three stories of gleaming hardware, patrolled by armed guards, and two tiers of aseptic offices where sober young men circulated among tribes and sub tribes of secretaries.

Spencer Foster's office occupied a great deal of the sixth floor. It was a private domain, a sacred place paneled in exotic wood, hushed by deep carpets, glowing with costly pictures and artifacts.

Although Jason spent hardly any time there, he and Jonathan had their offices in the west wing of the same building, quite a long way from Spencer Foster's east wing office. The outer room was dominated by a woman of indeterminate age, a sort of secretary-cum—receptionist. She was English and after years in America, still spoke with the distinctive English accent that is an asset for secretaries in America. There were two guards, one of whom conducted visitors through the silent corridors, while the other stood watch and warded off intruders. Spencer's father had founded the empire by first dealing in military surplus.

Fortune begets fortune and the old man never seemed to lose his touch. He put the money he made from the trade that flourished for a couple of years after the war into land and cattle. There must have been the underlying love for land and cattle that appears in all Texans' hearts, leading to the fancy cowboy boots and hats. But there was money to be made in beef, and when some oil was discovered on one of his properties, old Jasper's fortune rose dramatically. When Houston saw its post-war boom Spencer's father sold the corner store that he had operated from for the astonishing sum, in those days, of close to $3 million and pumped the money into shipping. In the years after the war, the tonnage handled by Houston, Beaumont, and Port Arthur increased more than those of New York, Baltimore, and Philadelphia, the nation's leading ports, and shipping along the Gulf Crescent was booming.

Of course, the Foster ships were not registered in the USA, but in Panama, a country that had such lenient laws governing conditions on vessels sailing under its flag that many ship owners registered their ships there, making its merchant marine the fourth largest in the world! Over the years, Fosters became a conglomerate involved in a clutch of businesses that ranged from cultivation of alfalfa and wheat, rearing of cattle, car dealership, oil, shipping, and construction. Just about anything that would make money.

Spencer did not quite have his father's legendary touch, but he was ruthless and what he lacked in intuitiveness he made up through cunning. There was no core competency or anything remotely like that in the group's thinking. Nor was there any thought given to business ethics. If Fosters had to bribe to get a contract, their executives went right ahead. Fosters was not averse to taking kickbacks from overseas contractors to whom it had parceled out subcontracts of contracts that it had bribed its way into getting. Of course it meant that the overseas country, and sometimes the US army, paid far more for the product or service than they should have. But Fosters found the system ideal. The money it received in such manner went into its slush funds, which could then be used for bribing others. If Fosters had to find out what its competitors were up to, it engaged industrial spies. And if it had to eliminate a rival, it was done. Of course they did not have the poor fellow killed, but he was finished off financially.

And, of course, Fosters had its battery of highly paid lobbyists in D.C. to influence the corridors of power. In the days after his father died, Spencer was involved in many dubious schemes. Investors lost money while Spencer invariably made a killing. His board members were also involved in it. Spencer just escaped being indicted and that was thanks to the high-priced lawyers and politicians on the Foster group's payroll.

But it scared him off similar schemes and he cut his business connections with the kind of people who ran scams and began to cultivate another breed of businessmen, the type who knew how to stay well away from the limelight and let the others take the fall if it came to that. That was, in any case, how big money was made, by skirting just outside the perimeter of the law and jumping back inside when the public were incensed and lawmakers got jittery.

Sometimes, though, as a result of a murky deal or two leaking out, its stocks took a hammering on the exchange. Then, too, Spencer made money by selling short. The SEC queried some of the sales, but it never had anything to pin on Spencer or his companies, for he never sold enough to create a big stir in the market and it was always through a slew of companies that were connected to Fosters but not subsidiaries of his flagship company. That summed up Spencer's attitude to life and business. He never spent a cent more than he should and always leveraged the situation to his advantage. Jonathan had known for long about the many politicians whom Fosters had cultivated, but he never sensed alleged plots or how his father made such a tremendous wealth. Jonathan had not worked in the company for long before he began to have a glimpse of the group's shenanigans. He remembered his father would tell the story that would express his opinion about the senators and how they are influenced by the big business.

"*A United States senator wields tremendous power and influence. Sometimes it can be even more powerful than that of the President. And do you know why? That's because his power is less visible. Everything that the President does is visible whereas a senator can reach into and have something done in virtually any department of government, as long as it is not illegal or something that might attract a lot of attention. That is why anyone in business or in the government will fall over themselves to do a senator a favor. It is a system of trades."*

Occasionally, Jonathan would ask Fred Warren in finance what was going on when he get suspicious. Fred Warren had been with Fosters for quite a long time and for as long as Jonathan could remember, he had always been friendly. But as he broached the subject, Jonathan was conscious of wariness in the older man's eyes, the earlier friendliness evaporating. The accountant's heavy eyebrows merged into a frown and at the end he stood up.

"Jonathan, I have enough problems here without having to answer these questions. And I don't know much. Now, if you'll excuse me…" Jonathan knew in a flash of intuition that Fred Warren knew everything that was going on. He also realized that the man wanted no part of it. All that he wanted at that moment was to get Jonathan out of his office.

Within the hour, Spencer called him in. He could still remember his father's words.

"Jonathan, Fred tells me that you have been inquiring into the African deal,"

"Yes dad. It seems to me that we have been giving a great deal of money to one N'kuma."

"I am aware of that. He is our agent there. You have to have somebody on the ground to represent the firm and to advise us. It's the standard practice."

"Yes, but $ 4million? That is an awful lot of money in Africa and he gets it just to represent us and give us advice."

"You don't know what it's like to operate in these countries. N'kuma has to spend a lot of money on various things."

"I hope it is not bribing." Jonathan murmured in a soft voice and scratched his cheek relentlessly.

"It does not concern you, Jonathan. Some things are best left alone," Spencer said with a finality that brooked no further comment and effectively ended the discussion. Thereafter, Spencer took many steps to ensure that Jonathan and later Jason, when he started working there a couple of years later, were not involved in or exposed to the murkier aspects of the business. There were far too many skeletons in that closet and some that could be resurrected one of these days, given the spate of scandals that had hit U.S. businesses and the government lately.

It was Spencer's penchant for secrecy that had initially prompted Jonathan to probe into some of Fosters' business deals. And when Spencer had called him and told him not to probe further, he wanted to get away from it all. Occasionally, he would think of a huge project—a system of dams and tunnels to direct water from the mountains to thirsty African cities and to generate electricity, and he was afraid with the thought of the penurious country that would be still further ruined by his father's projects that cost at least twice the true estimates.

Nevertheless, decisions were always made by his father and his confidants and he would rarely seek out any suggestions from his son. Jonathan was often perplexed by this decision but realized that Foster holding was not run ethically. Aren't the some unethical rich people who made their money in a corrupt way creating the system of inequality and keeping it working in their favor? He questioned that more often.

That's why he wanted to promote social transformation with fiery social conscience and a deeply felt belief in society that would bring out the healing. He would like to prove that giving can be a part of one's activism. He wanted to use his wealth to build a better life for others without taking lot of help from Government. He knew Government is neither enemies nor friends but they need each other. He was frustrated and disparaging and disapproving when he saw the difference was growing even more between the classes - the poor and rich. It was not that he wanted to make everyone rich —it would never be possible - but he could provide all the assistance what he could spare to make their lives a little bit better and happier. When he earned enough money by working for his father he would start his own business and he would be able to provide something for the needy. That one thought was crossing his mind over and over again now.

Of course the younger Fosters, Jonathan and Jason, were always inducted on the board of the parent company. Jonathan remembered quite clearly the first board meeting he had attended in the hushed boardroom with the long mahogany table. These meetings were largely ceremonial, and with outside directors present, the agenda had nothing other than reviews, budgets, and the statutory items. Jonathan knew that the real decisions were taken elsewhere—in the quiet confines of Spencer's paneled and book-lined office.

Over time, however, he got used to working in the company and then had no desire to probe any more. He had by then realized that it may be better not to know everything and there was no profit in knowing all that was going on. Of course, should he ever be called upon to give evidence, he would painfully but truthfully share the knowledge with the authority. That thought would bring devastating, excruciating, and agonizing feelings in his stomach. Perhaps that was why his father had not let him into everything Foster Holdings Inc was up to.

After his marriage to Oliana and the exposure to the pure lifestyle in Hawaii, Jonathan began to think a lot more about what he wanted to do with his life. Money was not an issue, and he could not understand why his father needed to go on making more and more money. There was nothing more that money could give the family. They had every conceivable luxury and extravagance, comfort, and lavishness in their life style. If his mother did not have something, it was not for lack of the money to buy it, but because she was not interested in it.

Jonathan often thought that people who are poor would steal to accommodate themselves. But he never understood why the rich would steal more and more when they did not need money. Jonathan was puzzled by the thought that how in the world people like Kenneth Lay, Kozlowski, and even his father could sleep at night when they were depriving middle-income and poor people and robbing their livelihood. -Where were their moralities?

Why did his father want even more? What was the point? If Spencer was scrupulously honest and conducted business with ethics, Jonathan would have given him all the help needed to go on expanding the business. He could even excuse it if the money the Foster conglomerate made was given in large measure to charity or for the public good. However, none of these considerations even touched Spencer Foster. He chased and made more and more, and in the process did not care who got hurt. Jonathan often thought that his father's way of doing business was a throwback to the days of the old robber barons of a century or more ago.

Why could his father not realize that it was an illusion to think that more comfort meant more happiness? On the contrary, happiness, Jonathan realized came out of the capacity to feel deeply, to enjoy simply, to think freely, and to cherish life, and to be needed. Material things only enhance life and provide an atmosphere, but they should not control your life, your overall thinking. He was happy and contented that he had Oliana to love. With her, after a long day at work, he found a peace that he had never experienced. With her, he could be himself, not this corporate being "One of these days" he told himself.

------

A few days later, he called his friend OC to join him for lunch. Like Jonathan, OC knew what big business was all about for he too had been born the son of a wealthy and successful businessman. His father, Amar Bose, had made a lot of money and was in every way as American as anyone else, although he had only come to the U.S. in the '70s. But he had, since then, acquired a doctorate in computer science from one of the leading universities in the country, an American wife, and U.S. citizenship. After working for a while in a couple of major corporations, he had gone on to establish a software company that was very successful in outsourcing work from the U.S. to India, the country of his birth. He was in every way as competitive as any of his American counterparts, and although his sense of business ethics was somehow better than theirs, his company was not required to use the shenanigans that had to be resorted to by some businesses.

Foster holding had a big cafeteria in the downstairs. Usually Jonathan had lunch in different places with clients but today he felt very restless in his mind.

He asked, "OC, I hope you would not mind if we have lunch in our cafeteria?" OC agreed with smile. Seeing Jonathan and OC, the manager came rushing to accommodate them in the best seats and engaged one of the waiters for their comfort. Jonathan ordered very little and said, "OC, I have to discuss something with you. It is confidential."

OC was curious. "I could not pinpoint what is going on inside this company. A lot of illegal activities, I presume, and I am afraid my father is involved in something illegal." OC wanted to make sure what Jonathan assumed had a solid basis. "Do you have any hard evidence?" OC asked with a doubtful voice.

Jonathan replied with dismay, "I only have a hunch that something is wrong."

OC smiled and said, "May be it is your imagination. You are working too hard. I tell you what, why don't you go out with Oliana this evening. Your mind will be at ease." Jonathan knew the only person who could ease his mind from this was Oliana. Lately, Jonathan was neglecting going out with Oliana as he was assuming more responsibilities. After shaking OC's hand, Jonathan said in a very relaxed voice, "You are right. This is an excellent idea, OC. What would I do without you?" They both laughed. He knew Oliana was his anchor. Her gentle touch and her Mona Lisa smile would take away the day's worn-out feelings.

— — —

Without wasting any time, Jonathan returned home earlier than usual and announced without any preamble that he was taking Oliana out to dinner. Oliana was surprised and pleased. She was suffering from despair. This might enable them to put a renewed loving relationship on a fresh foundation, Oliana thought. It had been quite a while since they had gone out together, just the two of them. She felt as if the leaden weight of misery, which had held her down for so long, had lifted. It would be an emotional reconciliation and bonding, which would renew their love. For the first time in several months, she felt her vitality returning—an almost heady excitement that the future might improve.

They both usually enjoyed Italian food, so Oliana wanted to go to the Grotto. They had not been there before. It was not one of those horrendously expensive restaurants that they were used to. Oliana thought that in an expensive restaurant she could not be intimate with Jonathan. She knew Jonathan was passionate, romantic, and believed in eternal love. All he needed was a reminder of their romantic past. She asked "Would you like to go to the Grotto restaurant? It's been well recommended as a warm place that offers authentic South Italian cuisine and traditional dishes from the Bay of Naples."

Jonathan was overwhelmed, "It is your day, my darling, whatever you say."

It was a lively restaurant, set in the style of a contemporary villa with brick arches, polished wooden beams, and star-like lighting. Jonathan felt every eye in the restaurant turn to watch him and his companion— mostly his companion— as they walked past *Il Furno*, the wood-burning pizza oven and the huge antipasto display. Oliana herself seemed immune to the attention, either unaware of it or accustomed to it.

They sat down in a private corner with a dimming romantic light away from the crowd and held hands. They gazed at the *Fellinesque* wall murals that depicted diners and masqueraders enjoying food and friends at a seaside until the *maitre de* produced the menu.

Jonathan was a bit of a connoisseur of wine and Oliana was used to him having lengthy discussions with the waiter. It therefore did not come as a surprise to her when after a long and animated discussion with the waiter; Jonathan turned to her and said, "I guess we're going to have to choose between *Amarone* and *Recioto*. Essentially they are the same except that *Amarone* is dry while *Recioto* is sweeter."

"If they are the same, how it that one is dry is and the other sweet?" she wondered and asked.

"They are both obtained from the vilification of dried grapes from the same vineyards. The difference lies in the process used and it is rather simple. They just stop the fermentation early to retain the natural sweetness of the grape sugar. It's the timing that makes the difference."

When the wine was poured, Jonathan raised his glass and said, "You look stunning today - absolutely stunning, my darling." Oliana looked radiant.

"What are you thinking?" Jonathan asked when he did not get any response from her.

"I was just thinking of how lovely it is here." She kept her hand on Jonathan's.

"Yes, looks like this place is really quite authentic. You feel as if you have been transported to a genuine *trattoria* on the Amalfi coast and most of all your love and your charming presence make this place even more beautiful," Jonathan said romantically. Oliana's achy heart started to pound. It has been a long time since Jonathan paid such a compliment and swept her off her feet. With happiness, Oliana started to squeeze his hands even more, and only stopped when she realized she was hurting him.

After a while, Jonathan glanced up from the menu and let his eyes rove all over the entire restaurant.

"Yes, it's quite a charming place. The *Oysters Mimmo* seems quite interesting," Jonathan said and read from the menu. "its Italian style fried oysters with lemon, garlic, and herb sauce. Would like to order that?"

"That should be nice," Oliana murmured. "What about *Scampi Grotto*. It's shrimp sautéed with mushroom, garlic, white wine and lemon."

"Yes, let's." They were both relaxed and felt like a newlyweds. As they waited for the appetizers, Oliana asked, "Surely you must get bored from time to time in the office. What do you do then, Jonathan?"

"When I get bored, I play mind games," he replied.

"Mind games? Like what?"

"Sometimes I think of the possible names that would result from a merger."

"Such as?" Oliana asked, not quite understanding what Jonathan meant.

"For instance if Federal Express and UPS were to merge, what do you think the new name would be?"

Oliana did not have a clue and looked at him quizzically and said, "Tell me."

"It could be FED UP," he chuckled.

Oliana too began laughing.

"What about Honeywell, Imasco, and Home Oil?" he then asked and then without waiting for an answer, said, "It would be Honey I'm Home!"

Oliana was pleased to see Jonathan in a jovial mood. It was so like him, she thought as she remembered his jokes about the slot machines when they were on their honeymoon in Las Vegas. She wanted the mood to continue and so asked him, "Do you have any more like that?"

"Yes, honey, 3M and Goodyear. Do you think you could work that one out?"

Oliana thought for a while and then it struck her and she said triumphantly, "Mmm Good."

"That's very good!" Jonathan exclaimed. "What about Swissair and Cheeseborough- Ponds?"

"Swiss cheese?" she asked hesitantly.

"Yes, of course!"

By then they had finished the antipasti and proceeded to study the menu for the *Pranzo*.

"I'm going to try the shell fish stew."

"Ah, the *Ciambatta di Frutti di Mare*. A traditional Neapolitan shellfish stew in an herbed *pomodoro* sauce served with pasta," Oliana said. "That should be good. I'm going to try the broiled snapper with seafood ravioli and cream sauce."

"That sounds good. Have you heard about the amazing pasta diet?"

"No, tell me"

"It worksa very well," Jonathan said, putting on an exaggerated Italian accent.

"You learn to walka pasta da refrigerator without stopping, pasta da cookie jar and pasta da pantry."

It took Oliana only a split second to get it and when she did she laughed until tears started streaming down her cheeks. "The love between us would deepen in time," she thought momentarily.

She leaned across impulsively and squeezed his arm and they relaxed into a friendly silence until the main course arrived. The stew and the veal arrived, piping hot and smelling delicious. After a moment's pause Jonathan said, "We must do this more often."

"Yes, that would be nice," she replied quietly, wondering whether they would have an evening like that in the near future. In fact, if anything, she felt vaguely afraid to think about the future. The rest of the meal, including a dessert of strawberry and ricotta angel-food bombe, was finished in relative silence. They were both seemingly caught up in the same mood, a romantic mood that lasted until he put his hand on her soft arm and said, "I guess it's time for us to leave."

More or less everybody had left by then. Oliana gazed at Jonathan in a mood of tranquil happiness. It had been a wonderful evening and one that she knew she would cherish for a long time. But she longed wistfully for the days when they had first met. Her thoughts took her back to Hawaii with its wonderful beaches and its balmy weather and a time when Jonathan was a stranger, friend, and lover.

# Chapter 9

The next day, Jonathan wondered what was afoot when, after being summoned by his father, he walked into Spencer's office on the sixth floor to find Fred Warren, Foster's head of finance, seated there at the conference table at the far end of that cavernous room. He was rarely summoned. He had been having difficulty persuading his father to get Fosters into the construction of low-cost housing, a project he knew would make a very little profit but which would give the group a much higher social standing in the community. He had not made much headway with Fred Warren, and the finance man was proving to be the main stumbling block. Was this meeting about that, and would he be able to get some concessions, he wondered.

His father stood by the large window, looking out at Houston's afternoon traffic. He turned around as his son entered the room.

"Good morning, Jonathan," Warren said, clearing his throat as he did.

"Good morning, Fred," Jonathan responded woodenly.

He had not taken to the dour and emotionless accountant and although with Warren looking after finance, he had had to work with him, he had never quite enjoyed the experience.

"Have you any idea why I called you here? Spencer asked.

"No. Is it about the housing project?" Jonathan asked, hoping against hope that it would be.

"No, it's not about your pet project, Jonathan. It is much more important. With our soaring costs, we can't afford to get into that kind of business, now. We need to cut down our cost of operation and that is what I wanted to discuss," his father replied summarily.

"Oh," said Jonathan despondently as he sat down.

His father sat down across from him and looking directly at him, said, "The time has come for us to outsource a lot of our work. We cannot go on like this. Our competitors have already gone down that path and if we don't we'll be in big trouble."

Jonathan was aghast. He had watched with concern while other companies, including General Electric, one of America's biggest companies, a company whose turnover exceeded the GDP of quite a few countries, had taken their work away from the U.S. to countries like China and India. He had often spoken out against this practice at various forums for he felt deeply that it was against the interest of the American working class. He never imagined that his own company would even contemplate being party to this.

"Dad, you've always said that you didn't want to outsource," he protested.

"I still don't want to. I don't trust the Indians and the Chinese. But it's either that or risk losing the lot of business in a couple of years."

"Surely that's a bit farfetched, isn't it?" Jonathan suggested.

"No." he shrugged. "Our competitors have been outsourcing their work for some time now. If we don't follow suit, we won't be able to compete even with the Europeans."

*In Pursuit of Love, Spirituality and Happiness*

"I guess that's true. But we'll have to lay off quite a few of our people if we do. Already there is a backlash."

"Perhaps. But the thing to remember is that there was a backlash a few decades ago when manufacturing was outsourced to places like China," Warren interjected quietly. "In reality, outsourcing transformed manufacturing from vertically integrated production structures to highly fragmented ones."

"What exactly does that mean?" Jonathan asked.

Fred Warren spoke again. "Fifty years ago, Detroit's River Rouge plant ate iron and coal at one end and simply spat out an automobile at the other. Now auto companies source components from a vast array of domestic and foreign suppliers."

"That's the problem. Americans lose jobs," Jonathan stated.

"Every new step in business brings about changes and people will have to adjust to it. Before Henry Ford turned mass production into the production of motorcars, more people were required to make an automobile. But did that mean Americans lost jobs? No. Eventually that made America the world's largest producer of motorcars."

"Henry Ford was a pioneer in mass production. Pioneers always pave the way."

"No. Henry Ford was not the pioneer of mass production. That honor belongs to Samuel Colt. It was he who was the pioneer of mass production. Henry Ford not only introduced the concept but made innovation of the assembly line process as well," Warren pointed out.

"I did not know that," Jonathan admitted.

"But the point is has American manufacturing become extinct since then? Hell no!" he said, thumping the arm of his chair. "Manufacturing production has risen by 40 percent over the last decade. In spite of lower wages abroad, foreign companies have chosen to produce cars made by high-wage workers here. Look at Honda in Ohio and Mercedes-Benz in Alabama. Then there's BMW in South Carolina and Toyota in California!"

"Fred, the problem with continuous outsourcing is that when all the companies go on outsourcing most of the jobs, who are they going to have left in the U.S. who can afford to purchase their products or services? Who will there be with enough money to buy their products?" Jonathan asked.

"That is only partly true, Jonathan. What you have to remember is that we are losing revenue on our container services. As you no doubt know, we have over 100,000 containers. The problem is one of insufficient use, which is why we are losing revenue. We require a Web-based system for tracking the container movement—a common interface to all our customers," Warren replied.

Jonathan knew that Warren was right. But deep inside he felt he should resist the move. He had such mixed feelings about the whole notion. Of course it may look good for Fosters, but was it good for America? That was what concerned him most. After all, Fosters had not yet had a bad year. Somehow the company had managed to keep its head well above water. But there had been a great deal of debate on this and he had heard both sides of the story.

"It's not in the company's long-term interest or that of its workers," he said hotly.

Out of the corner of his eye he saw Fred Warren rolling his eyes and mumbling something about interfering goody two shoes.

"Jonathan, it is in the company's interest. Of that I am certain. As for the workers, let me remind you that the company owes its workforce only the paycheck they earn and a clean working environment. It does not owe them a job! Our duty is primarily to our shareholders and therefore anything that improves our bottom line is in the interests of the company," Spencer said vehemently. "The House of Representatives has just passed a bill to block export-import bank loans to companies that have moved their offices overseas," Jonathan stated.

"Let me remind you, Jonathan, that we are not shifting our offices. Fosters will remain a true blood American corporation," Spencer said, trying to keep his temper under check.

"Eventually we may be left with only the headquarters in America."

"No, Jonathan. Not in our kind of business. Only a lot of clerical and routine work will be done outside the U.S.," Spencer countered, with mounting irritation.

"The fact remains that there may be short-term losses for some, but there will be long-term gains for almost everyone," Fred Warren chimed in.

"How can that be?" Jonathan asked.

"Well, manufacturing jobs have been migrating out of the U.S. for decades. In the '90s a booming economy and a boost in the services kept a lid on this," the finance man replied.

"It was not just because of that. There were other factors that made it so and you know it Fred," Jonathan countered.

"Perhaps, but when IT operations and other general activities are sent to a low-wage country like India, it can reduce the costs by anywhere up to 40 percent. Thus, keeping the inflation in check and maybe increases a company's profits, allowing it to invest in growth. That is what may create jobs in that company," Warren replied.

Jonathan, although he did not let anything register on his face, was intrigued by his role in all this. He had only a lay person's knowledge of information technology. Why he was being drawn into something like this, he wondered. "What is it that you want me to do in this, I don't understand?" he finally asked.

Spencer leaned across the table towards Jonathan and said, "It is not you so much, as your friend, the Indian chap, whom we need."

"OC? What about him?" Jonathan wondered what was to follow.

"He's partly Indian, isn't he?" Spencer asked.

"Yes. His grandfather is an Indian, but his mother's side of the family is true-blue Americans." Jonathan knew his father wanted to hear that.

"That's wonderful," Spencer admitted.

"We would like your friend to visit India and check out a couple of IT companies and see if we can get one with exposure to and experience in our line of business."

"Yes, I'm sure he would. He's in that line of work anyway," Jonathan replied.

"Then that's settled. Can you fix up an appointment sometime next week?"

"I should imagine," Jonathan replied, a bit scared and anxious that it would be his friend who would spearhead the group's foray into outsourcing of work.

– – –

A warm feeling crept over Jonathan when he saw OC at the doorway. All his inherent disgust with this corporate world and its shenanigans disappeared when he looked at this tall, slim, almost ascetic-looking friend of his. OC was as fair complexioned as any full-blooded American and it was only his large dark eyes—slanted, olive eyes—under drooping eyelids that gave him a melancholy look, that gave any hint of the Indian in his ancestry.

There was a kindness and gentleness in his countenance, which endeared him to a lot of people. He could not hurt a living creature. Jonathan knew, however, that in spite of his gentleness there was a fierce side to OC, which emerged in his struggle for faith. He had wrestled with it for years and it was only of late that he had come to terms with it. He looked quite content with life as he stood there at the entrance to Spencer's office.

"Come right in," said Spencer, getting up and shaking hands with the young man. "OC, isn't it? May I call you that?"

"Well, that's what I'm called by most people," OC replied, shaking the outstretched hand.

"What then is your real name?"

"Well, its Ashish Bose, pronounced like Oshish. My grandfather, as you perhaps know already, is from India. That's why I got landed with this name. But my mom couldn't get around to pronouncing it and began calling me OC and it's now sort of stuck and I sort of like it," OC replied with smile.

"Please, sit down," Spencer said indicating a chair around the table.

When OC was seated, Spencer said, "I guess Jonathan has briefed you about our situation."

"Yes, he has. But I need more specifics," the young man said, as he pulled out a large leather diary from his briefcase.

"Yes, we'll provide all that you'll need. But I need to know from you what your feelings are about outsourcing," Spencer replied as he looked intently at the young man.

"I guess it's inevitable. But every country has to start somewhere and what is one country's gain is often another's loss. The British, once they colonized India, put a country that was a leader and a pioneer in areas such as textiles, manufacturing, and the sciences into a backward cycle. But they had to strive to become such a power, as indeed America had to, once upon a time."

"What do you mean?" Spencer could not help asking this question.

"Well, the fact is, the American cost of living is too high to compete at the international level and with trade barriers coming down, the market is wide open and American companies have to focus not just on protecting their domestic market, but finding products that can find markets outside of the U.S.," OC replied, "Well, the competition can sometimes be frightening. Do you know that the average pay of one American programmer can pay 10 Indian programmers?" OC asked with a glimmer of a smile.

"As much as that? Spencer asked.

"But won't it slow down the growth of talent within the U.S.?" Jonathan asked.

"No. The U.S. still offers the best university education in the world and talent from all over the world is drawn to these shores," OC replied, nodding his head.

The truth was that Jonathan identified with OC to a great extent. Like him, OC felt a bit estranged from the manner in which his father Amar Bose operated his business.

"Well, then, let's forget about the dilemma and come to the problem on hand," Spencer replied with irritation.

"Of course," OC replied.

"You have a good idea about our business, don't you?"

"Yes. Over the years, Jonathan has filled me in on a lot of things about Fosters," OC replied, but his face mirrored his curiosity.

"Good! Then I don't have to give you the broad picture. What we require essentially is a Web-based system for tracking the container movement with a common interface to all our customers," Spencer said.

"You are a large operator. I understand that you have over a 100,000 containers moving around the country. You should have gone for such a system long ago," OC replied.

"I guess you're right. But then it's perhaps better late than never. Do you have any recommendations?" Spencer asked.

"Yes. India has quite a few top-notch IT companies. TCS an acronym for Tata Consultancy Services, Wipro, and Infosys are the ones that come to mind. But there are a few others that are making great strides," OC replied.

"Which one would you recommend?" Fred Warren asked as he eyed OC skeptically.

"TCS is privately held by the House of Tatas, which you may know was for long the biggest business group in India. TCS has recently gone public with an issue that netted them over a billion dollars. The issue was oversubscribed more than five times!"

"Then who would you recommend?" Spencer asked.

"I would recommend Prowin. It's a new outfit, but it's on a fast track right now," OC replied.

"Who have they worked for? Any big names?" Warren asked.

"Well, they've worked for quite a few of the Fortune 500 companies. More importantly, although I have not worked with them, I have seen some of their work and it is good. They are located in Bangalore." The conversation ended as OC got up from the chair to say good bye.

– – –

Two weeks later, OC left for Bangalore, India, a land of many mysteries and fascinations. The tallest mountains – snow-covered mighty Himalayas, world's largest and oldest democracy, the silent spirituality with amazing wealth of wisdom and culture made India a mystic land of mediation, contemplation, and enlightenment. Jonathan thought how lucky OC was. If he was not so busy with his recent housing complex projects he would have gone to visit India with Oliana to see that mysterious, religious, ancient land that he had heard so much about from OC. He remembered when he was very young how exciting it was when he could go on a cruise with his parents, as his mother would never permit him to visit any place without them. He remembered his childhood was smooth and exuberant, and he did not travel much – he had the luxurious lifestyle to compensate for it but in his long and desperate desire, he wanted to visit other countries, like India, China, Europe, wanted to know the different culture- different than his. He wanted to taste the different food, different life style as all young adventurous Americans do. But it never became a reality as one after another responsibility always consumed his time.

# Chapter 10

Bangalore, capital of India's southern state of Karnatak, is a curious mix of cultures. It was once a cantonment town and the presence of the army and air force are visible everywhere. There was a time when it was the preferred place for retirement for officers of India's armed forces and the watering hole of plantation owners. There was a time when it was a lovely city full of trees that lined its broad and well-kept streets. There was a time when it was referred to as the Garden City. There was a time when it was a quiet place of old money and army discipline. At 2,000 feet above sea level and set on the largest plateau in the world, it was once a cool place in the summer.

It was no longer so. The change started with the influx of people from Bombay who, taking advantage of Bombay's real estate being among the most expensive in the world, sold their tiny apartments in India's biggest metropolis for princely sums and bought large apartments in downtown Bangalore, with cash to spare and more. That set the trend for Bangalore's construction boom, which in turn made it a concrete jungle, a far cry from its earlier sobriquet.

Then came the software boom, which changed the place beyond recognition. Bangalore became almost overnight India's answer to Silicon Valley and with that Yuppie land. Yuppies had spending power and bought everything on credit. The old Indian habit of saving and building assets was not for them. It was not that thrift was impossible; it had become unfashionable. For them the necessities of life were food, clothing, shelter, and credit cards.

That was the Bangalore that OC flew into to scout out a software company for Fosters. As he stepped out of the airport, he could feel the blast of the noonday heat. In the air-conditioned car that had been arranged for him, it was no better until they were well into the city and the air-conditioning came to terms with the heat of the metal on the car.

"Is it always likes this?" he asked the driver.

"Sometimes more bad," the driver replied as he maneuvered the vehicle through the crowded street. It was only when OC stepped into the magnificent teak and marble lobby of the West End Hotel that he finally felt comfortable. He remembered a brochure describing this old hotel as two stories high and 20 acres wide and thought that the copywriter had it just right.

It had been a long haul from Houston across the Pacific and almost all of Asia, and OC was tired. Even the comfort of first class had done nothing to take away the exhaustion. So after checking in and walking across to his suite just across the pathway from the reception, he soaked himself in lukewarm water in the bathtub and then dropped off to sleep.

– – –

Prowin's offices in Koramangala, one of the newer of Bangalore's suburbs, were housed in a modern building of glass, steel and concrete. The furniture was modular. "Must be Swedish," OC thought to himself as he was guided through the office to the conference room attached to the office of Prowin's Chairman, Mahesh Vatsa.

Mahesh Vatsa, got up, looked at him strangely, and extended his hand in greeting as OC walked in with Ravi Narayan who as Prowin's executive director operations was effectively the company's second in command. OC had already experienced that at the immigration counter, at the West End Hotel, and Prowin's reception. Even Ravi Narayanan had a puzzled expression on his face when he met OC for the first time, a few minutes before. He was a bit surprised that Ravi Narayanan had not made any comment though about the incongruity of the name on his business card and his appearance.

"Please sit down," Vatsa said indicating a leather-upholstered chair. OC sat down and it was no surprise to him that he found himself flanked by the men from Prowin. Although they were about the same age, Ravi Narayanan was the taller of the two. Both had a similar clean-cut bespectacled looks. They were dressed rather dapperly and bore the mark of financial success on their bodies.

"Ashish Bose. That's a Bengali name! You don't look like any Bengali I've seen," Vatsa began.

"I guess I should have told you when I called. But then it doesn't make much of a difference. Does it?"

"No, it doesn't," Vatsa conceded. "But we are a bit intrigued."

"Yes, as is everyone in India who sees my card and me at the same time," OC replied with a smile.

"Yes, to most people it would appear as a bit of a mismatch," Ravi Narayan offered.

"I can imagine. I've always had some difficulty explaining my name. You see, my grandfather is a Bengali, but the rest of my ancestry is white American," OC explained.

"I guessed as much and I didn't ask or say anything earlier because I knew you'd have to repeat it for Mahesh's benefit," Ravi Narayan stated candidly.

"Gentlemen, I think you know what brings me here," OC said after the preliminary introductions and pleasantries were done.

"Yes, of course," Mahesh Vatsa replied. "Your e-mail gave us a good idea."

"I know that you provide comprehensive IT solutions and services including systems integration, information system outsourcing, package implementation, software applications, development and maintenance, and research and development services to corporations globally," OC volunteered.

"Yes we do, but we have some recent good news to share with you," Ravi Narayanan announced.

"Oh, a new development?" OC asked.

"Yes," he said proudly.

OC was impressed. He was pleased that he had decided on Prowin even before the IT company had given him news of the new accreditation. That made his selection all the more a professional one.

"My client is a large inter-nodal service provider supplying equipment such as containers to large railroad consortium in North America, Canada, and Mexico," he began.

"And what exactly are the issues you wish us to handle?"

"There's quite a bit but essentially, at least as I see it, there is an acute problem of insufficient use of my client's containers and that results in reduced revenues."

"Why is that so?" Vatsa queried.

"Lack of information as to where the containers are is at the root of the problem," OC replied.

"Where do you think the problem lies?" Ravi Narayanan asked.

"Well, it would appear that the information lies in islands which are not accessible to the people in the field. The company therefore requires a system that allows the design and the operation teams' real-time access to their mobile assets, which are the containers. Can you handle something like that?"

"Well, we have."

"That's similar to my client's requirements," OC murmured.

"Yes, I think so, too. On the face of it, I should imagine that what your client requires is a Web—based-system that will track the containers across inter-nodal ranges with a common interface to all railroad customers."

"Yes, and it would have to be made available irrespective of platform differences."

"That could be arranged."

"My client also requires an effective billing and collection system with provision for network alerts and support for over a thousand users."

"That is the least of the problems. We should be able to handle the job without much difficulty," Vatsa declared.

"The bigger problem is getting a U.S. visa for our personnel who have to go to America," Ravi Narayanan stated.

"That's always so, but it's not an insurmountable problem," Mahesh Vatsa stated.

"Then it's settled. We can work together, can we?" OC asked.

"Yes, we just need to agree on the financials," Ravi Narayanan stated.

"Yes, please send your quotation to Fosters in Houston. They can take it from there."

Ravi Narayanan gave his charming company to see OC off; probably he wanted to talk to OC in private. "I hear there are hot debates going on in your country about outsourcing in India and China. Our country, at this moment, only provides information technology at very cheap prices, and I know it is providing our huge population some jobs and for China, it's creating a middle class.

America needs a market to sell its product—in the long run India and China need to buy more goods from America with the money they

*In Pursuit of Love, Spirituality and Happiness*

are earning. If the American government plays its card right, they will export more and that will create jobs for Americans. OC agreed with the view of this wonderful gentleman.

Ravi Narayanan continued, "Maybe it is time for American companies to create a balance, keeping some manufacturing jobs for luxury goods, specialty goods, and innovative goods where consumer will pay high prices in America and sending jobs for cheaper goods overseas." OC never thought that way. Ravi Narayanan continued, "I shall not say but come to think about it, I mean, with this outsourcing practice—an Indian software engineer or programmer gets some money to live adequately, but not lavishly. At the same time, American programmers are not making huge amounts of money—the people getting richer through the outsourcing are the company itself. May be they will invest more. Don't you agree, OC?" OC agreed. "America has so many resources, talents and innovative powers, that's why I do not understand why they do not use that for their advantage. We only see the gun culture, violence, and sexual appetite in TV. We see in the television and we believe in it. Is it true?"

OC always saw the problem with the western eyes. Now he had to see the solution with the eastern mentality. He had seen both worlds and he knew that one day America has to understand that they are part of the same world.

– – –

OC returned to the hotel and spent the rest of the day staring out at the garden outside his room. 'Was it always spring here?' he wondered, as he looked out the window at the profusion of flowers in the garden and remembered that the brochure had assured him that every room in the hotel overlooked a garden.

There was nothing left for him do in Bangalore. He decided to go to the ashram of Shree Shree Ravishankar, the blithe spirit behind the Bliss Foundation that had made a lot of waves, particularly in corporate circles around the world, with its Art of Living Courses. He called up the center and after being told that the guru was out of the country, decided to proceed to Calcutta, or Kolkata as they called it these days, and visit his precious grandfather.

It had been a long time since he visited his grandfather. He always wanted to visit him but moving all over the country for the company prevented him. Now that he was in India, he wanted to give a surprise to his grandfather with a visit and spend time with him as much as he could. He wanted to go to Belur Math straight where his grandfather spent most of his time. OC thought that when he visited his grandfather he would seek some advice about Jonathan. He was very worried about Jonathan, and though he pretended that he was not aware of any wrong doing by Spencer, he had some suspicions about all the dealings in the corporate world. In time, he thought he would approach his grandfather with this problem. "Who could be more expert in conventional and un-conventional wisdom than his grandfather?" Though OC looked different than his grandfather, there were more similarities than differences in their personalities.

# Chapter 11

Sprawling over several acres of land on the western bank of the River Hooghly, a distributaries of the holy River Ganges, the *Belur Math* in Calcutta, India, is a place of pilgrimage for people from all over the world, even those professing different religious faiths. Because of the peace it exudes, it is also a place where even people who are not really interested in religion come. Few years ago when OC visited Belur Math in West Bengal he saw many visitors from England, Germany, France, America and many westerner came to pay tribute to Ramakrishna mission and it did not change at all after all these years. As a matter of fact it grew its membership more than before. O.C was wondering about that as he was not an exception either. He was craving for another outlet to connect to the spiritual world and he knew he came to the right place where he felt the inner peace. People all over the world found the connection to spirituality here. Ramakrishna mission known as "Vedanta Society" are present in many cities in America, now, like

New York, California, to name a few. O.C. visited them often when ever he had times between works.

The Ramakrishna Order of monks, which had come into existence in 1886, was originally housed in an old dilapidated building at Baranagore on the eastern side of the River Hooghly, West Bengal. India. In 1938, the Belur *Math* premises, which include the main monastery, several temples and the headquarters of the twin organizations of the Ramakrishna *Math* and the Ramakrishna Mission, were sanctified by Swami Vivekananda, Sri Ramakrishna Paramahansa's greatest disciple. As a matter of fact, Gandhi formed his philosophy on the teachings of Ramakrishna principle. O.C. was aware of that.

After his grandmother's death and his only son's departure to America, OC's grandfather decided to stay in close touch with Ramakrishna Mission's Belur Math on the banks of the Hoogly River where he found his peace and tranquility.

As always, whenever OC entered the hallowed grounds of the abbey with his grandfather, OC was overcome with awe at the serenity that pervaded the place and the beauty of the buildings. The *math* itself had a unique style. The Swami had wanted the *math* to reflect and embody the spirit of religious fraternity. And it looked as if he had succeeded in that, for although there was a hint of the Gothic, particularly at its entrance, its turrets and domes made it look like a temple, a mosque or a church depending on the way you looked at it.

Now as he stood with his grandfather on the lawns of the *math*, OC remembered his grandfather's words.

> "*The Ramakrishna Order stands as a symbol of the eternal truths of religion tested and embodied by Sri Ramakrishna and Swami Vivekananda and their message of harmony of religions, divinity of the soul, renunciation and service. It is free from bigotry and sectarianism, rational and modern in outlook.*"

He had known quite a bit about the all-pervading caste system in India and had once asked his grandfather whether there was more bigotry in Hinduism than in other religions.

> *"Bigotry is there in all religions. As long as man is ego-centric and thinks only of his own power, it will be there. Such people often use the mantle of religion to clothe their bigotry. Do you know in some temple, here, the priests forbid the person with other religion or sometimes even the lower castes to enter, which is another form of bigotry?"*

As OC read in the newspaper about the hostilities between Christians and Hindu nationalists, he could not help asking this question. In Bhubaneshwar, hundreds of Christians, fearing more clashes with Hindu nationalists, fled to government-run relief camps where authorities on Saturday were providing them with food, medicine, and security. The clashes left at least four people dead including three killed when police fired on a group of hard-line Hindus that had torched a police station in Kandhamal district's Brahmangaon village. The killings and subsequent flight of nearly 700 Christians to four relief camps are the latest in a series of religious and political power struggles in the secular but Hindu-dominated India's eastern state of Orissa, which has one of the worst histories of anti-Christian violence. In 1999, an Australian missionary and his two sons were burned to death in their car in Orissa following a Bible study class. Since Monday, Hindu nationalists have ransacked and burned about 19 churches, according to officials who say Christians burned down several Hindu homes in apparent retaliation.

But relations between religious minorities such as Christians who account for 2.5 percent of the country's 1.1 billion people are usually very peaceful, only in few places the problem exists.

What about the Ramakrishna Order?" OC asked impatiently to his grandfather.

*"The math and its missions around the world are different from other Hindu organizations. It is committed to the task of ushering in a new age in which distinctions of caste, creed and class do not exist. And in which man reaches fullness in God and all his activities are carried out as an act of worship."*

"What is it about this place that makes you feel at peace with the world?"

OC asked as he gazed at the buildings.

OC's grandfather was surprised and pleased to see the depth of knowledge he had acquired and it made him very satisfied with his grandson's curious mind.

*"It is a place of pilgrimage for people from all over the world, even those who profess different religious faiths. That is why there is peace here for even people who are not really interested in religion come here seeking peace."*

*"But doesn't one have to accept Sri Ramakrishna's philosophy to find true peace?"*

*"Not really,"* his grandfather replied. *"You have to reach a stage of realization in which you see that all religion is basically same."*

OC assented quietly as he gazed out over the river in the setting sun. He enjoyed these discussions with his grandfather. *"Actually Ram Krishna believed that all religion preaching are the same message of tolerance, equality and love towards each other and that's why Ram Krishna's preaching attracted me so much."* He explained more. *"You do not have to leave your family and loved one to acquire God—he preached. Though the Guru or "Sannasi" leave everything earthly and goes to Himalayas to get in touch with the higher power—he does not need any idol or images but for the ordinary people who cannot reach that stage need some concrete images to concentrate their minds. There is only one God but there are many religious paths to reach God."*

Having spent some time in America, his grandfather knew what he was talking about and he brought into their discussions so much of what he had experienced in America without compromising his belief in Vedanta. It thereby brought so many things into focus. OC felt a glow of divine touch in his heart, too. He was looking for some answer for Jonathan as well. Maybe his grandfather's wisdom would provide that in time.

By then it was time for the evening *aarti* ceremony, which would be followed by prayers. Suddenly, OC noticed a young woman crossing the other veranda symmetrical to one he was on. She was so quick to disappear that OC only could spot portion of the sari, which was the traditional dress for Indian woman, wrapped around her swan-like neck. She appeared like a dream and vanished afterwards. OC wanted to ask his grandfather about the young mysterious woman but he noticed his grandfather was already transformed into a spiritual state. Grandfather and grandson entered the portals of the abbey and proceeded to the prayer hall to join the monks in the evening prayers.

---

The next morning after his daily meditation, his grandfather came down to the balcony from where OC was looking at the everyday way of life of average people in Calcutta. There was so much air pollution that he could barely see any of the activities that were going on the road – the chaos -the hustle and bustle of the carts, trucks, Rickshaws and cars, but amazingly most of the people still were peaceful. Many thoughts were traveling through his mind. The question he had never asked, today he wanted to ask for an answer. He was thinking about that for a while.

"How do you feel about Christianity?" asked OC to his grandfather as he stood beside him. A warm tranquil glow passed over OC's grandfather's face as he knew where the question was coming from. OC had adopted Christianity from his mother's side. His grandfather was comfortable with OC's adaptation of Christian religion, though people with an extreme view would object and show intolerance. Most of the Hindus have tolerance and understanding of Christian religion as it has many similarities. Lots of upper class and well-known figures in Indian society accepted "Bramho" religion, which is similar to Christianity.

"Why don't we discuss that after breakfast," Grandfather suggested as they were heading to the breakfast nook. As they were leaving the balcony OC spotted the young woman again on the side street as she was getting into an old mid-size car and drove away. OC's grandfather noticed the wonder in his grandson's eyes – the eyes of praise, the eyes of amazement, the eyes of surprise, and speculation.

Before OC would ask any question about her, Grandfather sensing his interest, made a remark with humor. "You must be wondering who that lady is! I notice your keen interest about her. You may not be aware that I observed you yesterday as well when you were exquisitely looking at her." OC felt a little shy about this whole matter. Grandfather ignored it and continued, "Her name is Sheila. She is an eye doctor – actually an eye surgeon – very dedicated and very efficient in her profession. She always visits the Belur Math to obtain the blessing of Goddess before she begins any surgery – that's why you saw her there."

Soon they entered the breakfast nook and sat down on the breakfast table. A male servant "Raghu" as his grandfather call him, brought some fruits, tea, and some breads and sweets on a tray. Grandfather said, "This is my grandson who came from America." Raghu's eyes became wider with surprise and though he could not figure out where America was, nevertheless assumed it must be a very faraway place and even wealthy as he looked at OC's expensive outfits. Grandfather smiled and said, "You have to take care of him." He did shake his head in shyness and left the tray on the table with shaky hands. They both started to laugh loudly. Grandfather then said, "Raghu, go to the Didi moni Sheila's house tonight and invite her tomorrow on my behalf to join us for the dinner." Raghu nodded his head in response. OC was glad that he would be able to meet this young woman who was creating so much fascination in his mind as he baffled for a while about how he was going to greet her or what he was going to say at the first meeting. In America, it was a straight forward matter – you meet someone, shake her hands, and then if you like her, may be, ask for a date –OC did that before. But in this case he was not sure at all – only one thing he was hoping for - she would like him and the conversation would be interesting.

Grandfather noticed that and smiled at him. Temporarily, he sifted all of his thoughts to other issue and proceeded to the library. He was amazed to see the collection of books—ancient books from China, authentic books, and special-edition books—books and books, on the shelves and everywhere in the library. He had never seen this kind of collection in his entire life. Books, he realized, were the source of his grandfather's passion, not to mention his intellect. He was a scholar from a well-known university. Grandfather took an encyclopedia called "Banglapedia" - a full knowledge reference and resources for scholar and students and started to read to satisfy OC's curious mind. "Indian philosophy was first laid out in the Upanishads, as you know. Upanishad is the fourth and final tier of Vedic literature, the sacred book for all

*In Pursuit of Love, Spirituality and Happiness*

Hindus. The 'Upanishad' literally means obscure knowledge, which is read with the preceptor in seclusion. But as the connotation suggests, the word refers to the special treatises written toward the close of the Vedic era in literature.

It reveals ways of getting rid of ritual complexities and contains subtle decisions on worldly rites of the early days and instructions on getting into a novel world of thought. Some Upanishads depict different aspects of contemporary social life. A few scholars believe that the knowledge of science was first manifested in the Upanishads from Vedic literature. The Upanishads do not deal with gods or goddesses; rather Brahma is central to the deliberation of the thoughts. They hold brief for the one Brahma as the centre of the universe: He is the Truth, the Conscious and the One worth Knowing; the rest is untruth, the ignorant, and the uninformed. The animate and Brahma are one, with no difference between them. Salvation of the conscious comes through the encounter with Brahma. And this, according to the Upanishads, is the sole objective of human life. But from around the 5th century BC, Hinduism began undergoing some changes. Following this period, a tendency to humanize the deities is also noticeable in that time, with the writers trying to ascribe human virtues and failings to the deities. In this way the deities, were brought closer to common human beings, who could try to emulate divine virtues described in Puranas literature.

Another difference between the Vedic gods and the gods of the Puranas in that time is that the Vedic deities symbolized abstract virtues and ideas, but the deities of the Puranas were regarded as real beings. Emphasis was therefore laid on visualizing and constructing their images. In this way, the importance of the Vedic deities gradually declined and the importance of the Puranic deities increased because of the manner of their worship.

In fact, each Puranas was composed to eulogize a particular deity and establish his or her worship. There were social and political reasons for this gradual change from the Vedic deities to the Puranic ones. Following the rise of Buddhism and Jainism and the invasion of India by Alexander (326 BC), Hinduism was in disarray. The widespread expansion and influence of Buddhism under the official patronage of the Maurya Emperor Asoka (3rd century BC) resulted in an even greater crisis for Hinduism. In an attempt to ensure that Hindus did not deviate from their religion under the influence of other religions, the leaders of the Hindu society laid down elaborate rites and rituals.

They also tried to propagate the doctrine of Hinduism in easy language in the form of stories so that the common people understood the religion better. This is why they composed the Puranas in the form of stories. The rites and rituals introduced through this literature became in due course the main forms of Hinduism."

OC listened very carefully and was charmed by this esoteric explanation. He had some knowledge of this subject. "It is so interesting. Now I understand many things but I still did not get the answer I was looking for."

"I am coming to that, just have some patience," grandfather replied after taking a pause. "During the 18th century, British rule was consolidating in India but the Hindu social systems were stagnating with too many traditional rituals and were exploited by the Brahmins (the priest) who wanted the power to their advantage to rule the people. At that time, Raja Ram Mohan Roy, a social reformer influenced by western thought, especially Christianity, found the need for a social reform and religious reform. Being moved by Christianity as he saw the similarity in early Hindu scripture of Upanishad, he started a religious movement where there is only one God, all-pervading and omnipresent and founded so-called Brahmo Samaj, which actually played a significant role in renaissance of India. Forgiveness and generosity to others governed his thought as it is in Christianity. At present, Brahmo religion is practiced in several Indian cities and in England. Now you can understand the basics of universalism and the similarity and how I feel about it." OC nodded his head.

"But we do not believe in idol-worship as you do." OC made a comment.

OC's grandfather took a deep breath and then said, "Well, we all personalize our God. Jesus is not in a distant place or abstract. You worship the image of Jesus - what Hindu philosophy refers to as an avatar, most commonly indicate the incarnation (bodily manifestation) of a higher being or the Supreme Being into planet Earth with the implication of deliberate descent into Lower realms of existence for special purposes like saving the mankind from destruction or sin, for the preservation of the just, and the establishment of righteousness. There are so many similarities and of course some dissimilarities between Lord Krishna and Jesus Christ and there is a long time relationship between these two religions. Many Hindus think Jesus is an Avatar. We portray Jesus surrounded by innocent children and nature."

OC wanted to know more about the Avatar philosophy and its influence as it appealed to him as a bridge between the two religions.

"The avatar concept was adapted by orientalizing Western occultism, specifically Theosophy. The theosophical society was the organization formed to advance the spiritual doctrines and altruistic livings known as Theosophy. Helena Blavatsky, later known as Madame Blavatsky, was a founder of the Theosophical Society. She immigrated to New York City from Russia. While living in New York City, she founded the Theosophical Society. Many researchers feel that much of New Age thought started with her. She came to India in 1879 and died in England in 1891. She was succeeded as head of one of the Indian Branch by Annie Besant, and W.Q Judge headed the American Section in California. You see, the primary objective of the movement was to bring about a universal brotherhood based upon the essential divinity of man. All religions are interconnected in this way and we exchanged our religious views long time ago with West."

Grandfather paused for a while and took some water to clear his throat. OC was waiting patiently for another explanation. Grandfather then started, "Idol worship or the idol images of many Gods and Goddesses for people in India represent all the goodness of the world, the many manifestations of God. But the idols that Christians think about now have a related story that happened many years ago." He grabbed another book from the shelf and read from it. "About 1300BCE, many Hebrews moved to Egypt to escape a famine. When the Hebrews did escape, tradition states that Moses, the leader of the Hebrews, divided the Red Sea for just enough time to allow the Hebrews to pass. Then God revealed the Ten Commandments to Moses, which formed the basis of Mosaic Law and are the model for both Jewish and Christian moral thought." Then he made his own comment. "But just before that, Moses was not certain that he had really found the promised land and people who followed him fell in dismay and in doubt and made all the idols with lot of gold and made themselves drunk and committed evil acts. Those bad idols represented evil things for the Hebrews.

As Christianity was derived from Judaism, it resulted in the idea that all idol worship is bad." It was unbearable for OC's grandfather to think that the Christian religion, being so great, could impose such constriction. He knew that the Catholic church embraced and gathered many statues, medals, relics, and artifacts as a sign of holiness unto the Lord God. The Catholic church always taught its followers to bow down before statues when in prayer. OC said, "How you can defend that when Exodus 20:4 declared that thou shalt not make unto thee any graven image." OC grandfather said "look at the word graven, it means bad images, not good images. I can challenge anybody who obeys Christian religion or any other religion to step on a picture or statue of Jesus Christ even though that is just a picture or statue. They would not be able to do that. Technically, they do not believe it but in real life they do. They are just searching. And to me it does not matter. The picture or the statue represents the real thing. There is no such thing as a false God. Hindus and all other religions approach the higher power through the good images and it all depends on the right interpretation." OC was relieved in his mind and went to sleep in peace.

---

The next morning, OC woke up very early, though it was not needed at all. He took the most expensive outfit that he wanted to wear that day to the cleaner and brought them back after a while. He wanted to look impressive to Sheila. The first impression would be the key to success of wining her approval. As he was waiting for Sheila, he had only one thing on his mind at that moment. It seemed to him that time was standing still for a long time. Finally the sun did set and evening came along. He was eagerly waiting for her and finally heard a knock on the front door.

*In Pursuit of Love, Spirituality and Happiness*

As usual, Raghu opened the door and showed her the way to the living room. Sheila entered with a box of sandesh - sweets that were customary to bring to the host. After entering the living room, she extended her hand to greet OC and said, "I heard so much about you from your grandfather." Then she apologized, "Oh, I am so sorry that I had to come little late as I had to work in a different hospital today that was a bit farther away." OC was a little perplexed at first and then later mystified as his eyes were captivated by Sheila's personality and openness. After the introduction, everybody took a seat and Raghu offered some tea, Somosas, and rasagolla. This was the first time OC had a proper glance at her.

She looked very smart and elegant with a beautiful georgette sari wrapped around her tightly – not sexy, but elegant. She had a fair complexion with a very sweet face and a beautiful smile. She had medium build and short hair. OC was charmed by her look. There was stillness for a while as OC was jotting down thoughts in his mind. Grandfather broke the silence and said to him, "You know Sheila has founded a charitable organization to take care of the poor who cannot afford to pay the fees for operations. It is so amazing that she takes care of the poor with so much care and love."

Sheila tried to intervene with modesty. "Well, it is not really that much yet, but I am trying my best to make it better. This is my passion. You know my father always wanted me to be the best doctor I could be and I am trying my best. I wish though I could do even more." The evening went very pleasantly with much conversation and laughter. Raghu served lamb curry, vegetable curry and basmati rice, dal and sweet chutney. Everybody enjoyed the meal. Sheila had to leave little early to join the meeting of her charitable organization, but they both wanted her to stay longer.

After her departure grandfather said, "Her mother always wanted her to marry but she was so busy with her doctorate degree and caring for the poor that she had no time to think about it. As a matter of fact, she went to England to take the training. Then when she came back she dedicated her entire life to that cause. I sometimes worry about her as she never takes care of herself." OC wondered about that too and was glad that she was not married. Two days passed by in whimper.

Gradually, in his mind, he was feeling some attachment to her but he was hesitated about making a phone call. Just that moment the phone rang. When she called, he knew that she must have liked him. It was a happy moment.

Sheila wanted to know if OC could join her at a function celebrated every year in this time of the year to remember the great poet of India, Rabindranath Tagore. He was hoping to see her, and this was the proper opportunity. It was exactly 6 o'clock she came to pick him up. While driving the car she sighed, "Oh! Do you see how dirty the roads are – the people in this country never think that they should keep the place clean – no civic sense at all! It was not like that before. The vegetable peels, dry flowers, paper bags, cans - you name it- all household garbage ends up in the street. People do not understand that this is the source of all diseases. Of course, over all poverty plays a role here as well." She looked very agitated and stressed.

To comfort her, OC said, "Yes, that's kind of true but people here are very nice and considerate and loving." Sheila agreed. Later she engaged in further conversation, "Do you feel that people are nosy here?" Do you feel that people are everywhere – no space? I know it is not like in America. You are not used to so many people- human explosion, isn't?"

OC laughed at the way she was expressing her thoughts, and then said "No, not at all, I think that they want to know more about my country. You know though we do not have this kind of problem but we have our own problem – drugs, guns, too much division."

A few moments passed in silence as they both digested the seriousness of the problems. Finally, Sheila said, "The place we are going to visit is called Rabindra Sarani where every year Bengali people gather to pay their respect to the great Nobel Laureate poet, recite his poetry, and also sing Rabindra Sangeets created by him that has an eternal appeal. He was probably the most prominent figure in the cultural world of Indian subcontinent and his multifaceted talent showered upon different branches of art, such as, novels, short stories, dramas, essays, painting etc – many defined by rhythmic lyricism, colloquial language, meditative naturalism and philosophical contemplation. Did you read his poetry?"

Though OC was more familiar with the popular culture, he had some knowledge about the classical culture and dance of Bengal as well.

OC said, "Yes. I know that he went to England and America. In 1912 when he went to England for the second time, he translated some of his poems from Gitanjali to English. The English poet Yeats translated most of the poems in English and wrote the introduction for Tagore's book. Tagore was awarded the Nobel Prize in 1913. The book created a sensation in the English literary world. From England, he sailed to America for the first time, went to New York and Chicago, delivered lectures at Harvard University and so on. He also founded a university in India, I know."

They both enjoyed the celebration. OC had a wonderful and eloquent experience about the Indian culture. After the function was over, they went to take some tea and snacks in a small café. OC said, "I enjoyed the dance and especially the recitation." Sheila wanted to hear that more than anything in the world. She thought to herself "if he understood the thought behind it he would not have any difficulty understanding me." They discussed many facets of the event in the car until they reached home.

They started to meet whenever Sheila was free. They took pleasure in each other's company and the discussion about many subjects. Every now and then they also went to see the classical Bengali movies and once in a while to the popular Hindi Bollywood movie. Often they went to Indian restaurants, since OC liked Indian cuisine, especially Tanduri chicken. They started to feel for each other. She wanted to explore the genuine way she felt about him – his big beautiful Indian eyes, the broad shoulders like the Americans – the combination of both appealed to her.

A few days went by in a joyful manner. Then reality set in- like everything it had its ending. She did not want to end the relationship but had to accept it as she had no other choice. Sheila knew that as her patients started to call her frequently. It also concerned Sheila when

OC declared that he was not a Hindu like his grandfather but rather a Christian. She knew that being in India it would be very difficult for her since all her family and extended family would not accept it. If she'd been raised in America, it would not even cross her mind to accept the marriage proposal immediately.

On the day before his departure, they were sitting on the bench in front of the lake–intimately, close to each other. They were looking at each other's eyes, sadly. The sun was about to set. There were some clouds blocking the sun and the sky was appeared to be a little dark instead of glowing-orange-red. OC's mood matched the darkness, the same as Sheila's. After a while, without saying a word, Sheila placed her hand over OC's. With this special touch they both knew what was on their mind.

A few moments passed by in silence. Eventually Sheila broke the silence and said sadly, "I really, really, like you. I have never met anybody like you. For a moment I thought maybe I would leave everything and go with you and maybe that would have been wonderful. But that is not the reality. Under other circumstances, it might have been possible but I have chosen my own destiny. I have committed my life to take care of the people who need me." She paused for a moment, she could not say anymore – her sweet voice choked with grief.

He looked at her. It was written all over her face - all the expression, her commitment to the other world, her decision to save the needy. Her eyes were filled with tears. She wanted to give so much but her patients were important to her as well. She said with hesitation, "The other day, a woman came to my hospital to talk about the surgery she needs. She is getting worse now. She is the sole earner of her family –she has to take care of her two children and she does not trust anybody other than me when it comes to her eyes. I gave an assurance that I would provide some assistance for her and to take care of the surgery. The problem is that it is far away from Calcutta, and I don't know when I will be back and may be by that time you have to leave. It is so sad that this is the way it has to be." It was a very hard decision for her. OC had to accept it with a broken heart as he knew that it was the right decision. They kissed gently and said to each other that they would never forget this special moment as long as they lived. Saying good bye was not easy but there was no other option, as the time was closing in.

After Sheila left, OC was prepared to leave India to go back to his home land, America. He was very sad about the departure, for his grandfather and for Sheila, but at the same time he was worried about Jonathan. He found out that Jonathan was having lots of problem with his father. He'd comforted Jonathan before departing America, but in the back of his mind he always knew something was troublesome. OC had to ask for the advice from his grandfather about Jonathan.

As usual, Grandfather was overwhelmed and replied, "You know the story of Kurukshetra in our epic book 'Mahabharata' where the prince Arjuna, the decorated warrior of that time, was confronted with the personal challenge on the battlefield. He was beset with doubt and could not see the reality. As you can see, the battlefield of Kurukshetra is symbolic of the enormous challenges in this world and Arjuna represents today's human being. Only when we regain intellectual clarity to overcome mental weakness and a firm vision of our duty in life then we fulfill life's mission. Tell the story and the advice I gave you to your friend and he will understand what I meant."

OC realized that this might be the ideal vision for Jonathan. For the last time he hugged his grandfather over and over again and felt sorrow that he had to leave grandfather, Sheila, and India behind. So did his grandfather. OC saw tears in Grandfather's eyes and he could not hold back his tears either. But it was time to go back home, America.

----

# Chapter 12

The power of a large corporation is enormous. Jonathan had experienced that in many ways. It is true that the good companies do contribute by providing good jobs, research facilities, and extraordinary technological and medical advances with their vision, But when greed comes along and ethical conduct is lost they ruin the lives of many people and environment and so called good companies get victimized by the bad corporations. Exploitation starts to deceive the poor in the name of capitalism. Jonathan remembered a conversation with OC just before he left for India. Jonathan kept hardly any secrets from OC, and OC was always by his side to help him out, as all good friends are.

They were discussing capitalism in connection with Foster Holdings because Jonathan was doubtful about his father's ethical behavior.

"I think that sometimes the capitalist political system is manipulated by some unethical corporations where they can get away with cheating, manipulating the books, showing profit when there is none, so called 'cooking the book,' lying to the shareholders and deceiving the general public. Do you agree with me OC?" OC agreed. He knew Jonathan was socially responsible and he also knew that Jonathan always wished for his father's company to be ethical and at or above regulatory standards in the areas of workplace safety and environment but in reality that was not the case.

Jonathan added sadly, "Think of today's CEO, for instance. They look good in front of the camera, they know how to persuade, and their presentations are perfect. What I mean is that they are like celebrities, a touch of glamour. Some of them even are treated like super heroes. I do not get it. Do you think they are really that and just think of their CEO pay package when the company is going under?" OC understood the reasons for Jonathan's anger and the passion he possessed for general public.

Jonathan added more as if he was talking to himself. "I have no problem when the company is making money, the CEO should be handsomely rewarded but when the company is going bust, they still are awarded with a handsome exit package and stock options with millions of dollars! Do you know how that is possible? CEOs keep the board members under their skin. Paradox, isn't it?" Lately, the corporate dishonesties were so visible that Jonathan could not help thinking of his father's corporation as well "The Foster holding." Large-scale bankruptcies, accounting scandals, corruption, falling stock prices, and heartbreaking news of retirees whose entire retirement has wiped out by misleading corporation are now every day's news.

Last night, Jonathan had very little sleep. He could hardly read the financial times on his way to work, but one of page caught his eyes. The financial editor, Mr. Cheng, wrote, "In just three years, they grossed about $3.3 billion before their company went bust, having wiped out hundreds of billions of shareholders value and net 100,000 jobs. Gary Winnick, founder and chairman of Global Crossing who grossed $512 m in 1999, a period in which Global Crossing lost 9.2 billion eliminated 5,020 jobs. Number 2 is Lou Pai—chairman of Enron's Energy Service Subsidiary, who grossed $270 million, needed to get liquid in 2000 because he left his wife for a topless dancer. Number 3 is Enron CEO Key Lay who, once admired, now dead, was charged with 11 counts of fraud. And the former head of Tyco, Dennis Kozlowski was accused of stealing $600 million, and remember that $6,000 shower curtain." He knew that would happen again and again when there were ethical violations. For a moment Jonathan was fearful for his father as he read the newspaper. Most of the companies behave ethically but handful of them not, including his fathers.

A bone-chilling thought passed through his spine leaving him frightened and petrified. Spencer Foster believed in the old saw that a corporation is an ingenious device for obtaining individual profit without individual responsibility. Although many of the companies in the umbrella of the Foster group were publicly held, he used the conglomerate that his father had built as his private domain. He realized that to succeed, one had to get the best deals. As he was fond of saying, *"Man is the only creature that bargains. No other animal does."*

Although he claimed that business was a combination of war and sport, it was more like war when he went after a company as a corporate raider. It was a no-holds-barred fight and he was not satisfied until Fosters had ground the victim into the dust and taken all the spoils.

*"You have to keep ahead of the conditions,"* he would always say. *"A trailer does not go very far."*

Spencer Foster's close friends were people like Martin Taylor, the multi-millionaire co-founder of Systems Company, Omega Torp Inc. Taylor had gone into forced retirement from Omega Torp because of tax reasons, but he was still a dabbler in real estate and investment schemes that interested Spencer. It was not just tax problems that had made Taylor quit the company he had co-founded. Like a lot of businessmen, he had skimmed along the edge of the law, preferring the spoils from the gray areas of legality, but for a reward that was high enough to warrant the risk. He was always willing to delve into lawlessness and then dart back again to his legitimate business. Taylor had occasionally been caught and was once convicted of fraud. Jonathan never got to know exactly what for, but it was a subject about which everyone clammed up.

Jonathan realized, however, that it had something to do with the stock market and the larceny of investment write off. One of his favorite quotes was oil tycoon J.P. Getty's immortal words, *"The meek shall inherit the earth, but not the mineral rights."*

Jonathan did not like the man. He was a real phony, the kind of person he would not believe even if Taylor had admitted that he was lying! He found him far too secretive and calculating and whenever he spoke to him he got the impression that he was filing away every bit and piece of information in that card-index mind of his for later reference. On more than one occasion, Jonathan told his father so. Spencer did not respond, but Jonathan knew from the glint in his eyes that it was not a question that he cared much for. It was clear that the two had a lot of common interests and that Spencer spent a lot of time with Taylor.

The man was clearly in touch with all that was happening in the world of business, particularly in the sunrise industries such as systems. He was someone who well knew the difference between being let in on a deal and being taken in on one. Spencer consulted him on a range of issues and from time to time made use of him, too. In one of his relaxed moments he told his elder son, *"You know my boy, in modern business it's not the crook you have to worry about, but the honest man who doesn't know what he is doing. That's why Taylor doesn't worry me."*

Another regular in the Foster headquarters was George Ayling. What he did, Jonathan never ever got to know. His father never brought up the subject and to the best of his knowledge, there was not a shred of paper or electronic communication that gave even an inkling of his background. As far as Jonathan could guess, all communication was direct. Perhaps that was why he was so frequent a visitor.

He was also rather unfriendly and his eyes never held a touch, not even a remote one, of a general air of greeting. He was tall but fleshy, with heavy jowls, soft lips, a cleft chin and receding hair, which was perhaps the only indication of the passage of the years. The only thing he had heard from OC that SEC had asked for an undisclosed amount of fine from him. The charge was that he had unjustifiably diverted million of dollars in his own fund. It was not criminal in nature; rather it was a civil complaint.

Was the man a criminal? If he was, why could he not get anything on him? These were the questions that Jonathan often asked himself. A completely different personality was James Dewey, once the whiz kid of broadcasting and movie production. He had mega-celebrity status and was known for his ruthless management techniques, which must have been what attracted Spencer to him. He had an imperious manner and his image was that of the original jet-setting swinger. He, however, had a casual sense of business ethics, which led to his downfall and eventual sacking from the major network he was working for. But he had walked away with millions of dollars worth of stock options, which he exercised. He had plunged immediately into the red-hot Houston real estate market of the time and the equally hot Wall Street stock market. He set up an import-export firm, which was successful because of the contacts that he had built up.

Dewey was prepared to enter into any deal that he thought would prove lucrative and was always sniffing ahead to the trends and shifts in taste. He had contacts everywhere, and Spencer often took him with him on his trips around the country and even overseas. Quite often they would get into deals together. Dewey, unlike Taylor, was a likeable fellow and Jonathan, although he knew exactly what the man had been up to, enjoyed his company. James Dewey was full of surprises and knowing that he had struck some sort of a chord with Jonathan, would often call him up and suggest meetings in offbeat restaurants and places like that where they would discuss a variety of subjects, very little of which had to do with business.

It was to him that Jonathan told everything about his problems in the office and it was from him that Jonathan got an inkling of why his father kept him out of all crucial business deals. "*In the takeover business, if you want a friend, you go out and buy yourself a dog,*" he once told him. "*That is why your father and many others like him have no friends in the world of business; they are all mere acquaintances. He isn't really close to any of them and clearly he doesn't want you to be involved in those deals any more than you have to. It's often better not to know.*"

It was also Dewey who suggested that Jonathan should take up golf.

"What's the point?" Jonathan asked. "It's just a waste of time."

*In Pursuit of Love, Spirituality and Happiness*

"It comes in handy when doing business."

"Really!"

"I'll tell you this. More businessmen play golf than any other game."

"Why is that?"

"Well for one thing, it gives you something to do while you're nailing down a business deal with all the potential businessmen."

– – –

Jonathan had seen the more complex side of his father at work, and watched him in tortuous long-term plans, making every kind of allowance for the vagaries of others. He could not see himself in any of those plans, but it puzzled him just the same.

He was angered by the bland and treacherous twists. But there was no choice. Jonathan often asked himself what he was doing in Fosters and why he worked so hard there when he had no reason to do it. He sometimes felt that his motive for working so hard was that at the time he had had something to prove. Was it to himself? Was it to his parents? That he could not say. But however unsure he was about his past, he was equally sure that it had nothing to do with his current emotional difficulties.

# Chapter 13

He remembered reading somewhere that if business kept a person so busy that there was no time for anything else, then there must be something wrong, either with the business or with the person concerned.

But what troubled him more than all this, however, was that he could sense that his relations with Oliana were deteriorating as he could not pay any attention to Oliana. He had expected that after being married for two years their marriage would settle down to a steady rhythm. To his chagrin, he found their inherent differences widening. It was not that she complained about anything. In fact, she never did, except to protest about some business party, which he too invariably wanted to stay away from. Nor was she distant. She was almost always friendly and caring with practically everyone they knew and in a myriad ways. It was to her that he first turned for anything. She also seemed to make it a point to look after him as best as she could. Often when Jonathan came home from work and after he had retired to the terrace out of the suite, as they always did, Oliana would mix him a scotch and soda and hand it to him and sit by his side. But her sixth sense would tell her that all was not well. She had an innate sense of his moods, even if he did not express anything. It had been the same all morning at the office. His mind was occupied with one occasion after he had stumbled across a transaction involving arms and equipment and the transfer of funds to the Cayman Islands. That's absolutely illegal.

She said, "I made it a stiff one," as she handed him the glass. "I think you need it," she said sympathetically. Jonathan could not help thinking about it—first there had been a meeting where he got some wind of the Cayman deal, then there was the memo meant for Fred Warren, which had inadvertently appeared on his computer screen, full of questionably wheeling and dealing Jonathan knew nothing about.

When he looked at her and she added, "You're still troubled by that. Aren't you?"

"Does it show, honey?"

"We've been married for two years now."

"The best two years of my life," he said with feeling and hugged her.

There was a silence. Oliana waited until he had sipped from the large Waterford tumbler of Bushmill's Single Malt in his hand. Then she said, "You still troubled by that?"

"I didn't say I am," he countered.

"No, you didn't. But I knew you'd tell me when you were ready. Do you want to tell me? Now?"

"Yes, honey," he said slowly. "Yes, I think I do."

"The Cayman Islands is a dead giveaway. Nobody does that unless there is something fishy going on." He thought to himself. And when he tried to tell her all about misgivings, of what was happening in the office and the shenanigans that he assumed his father was up to, he could not. He tried hard to tell her everything but he resisted as he knew that it would be too much for her, sweet Oliana—he did not want to overburden her with these enormous, disgraceful, and outrageous problems. She should not be smudged with all the deceitful, scandalous occurrences what were going on in the Foster Holdings. He was ashamed of his father's deceitful act.

"Why don't you just chuck it up? You can do just about anything you want with your life, Jonathan," she suggested looking at Jonathan's troubled face.

"Yes, I know. But I can't just stand by and not be involved. As I've told you before, Dad needs me, particularly when he's away." Jonathan looked worried.

"Jonathan, you are invaluable to your father, but you must not make the mistake of thinking that you are indispensable." She wanted desperately for Jonathan to be happy again.

"It's not that I think I'm indispensable. I know I'm not," he murmured again.

"Then why don't you refuse to do those things which you don't like to do?"

"I once asked dad that and do you know what he told me?" he asked.

"Tell me," she suggested.

"He said, '*You're not here to refuse.*' Of course he was right. As long as I'm there, I can't refuse."

"But do you want that, I know you won't be happy?" she asked, her eyes searching his face.

"I don't know. I am thinking that all the time"

"And he does not keep you fully in the picture."

"I've thought about that too. I think maybe dad does that more to protect us."

"What does that mean?" she asked, not quite understanding what he was saying.

"Well, what I don't know won't hurt me." Jonathan flipped the magazine pages as he was having the conversation and looked away. Oliana could sense that Jonathan wanted to end the discussion as it was not going anywhere.

"You've changed a lot in these two years, my love," Oliana uttered looking at her absent-minded husband.

"Have I?" he asked, puzzled at her words.

"And, remember, life is too short to be unhappy." She wanted to alert him. Oliana waited for a while to continue with the conversation but Jonathan was deeply absorbed in his own thoughts. Oliana realized that Jonathan wanted to be left alone. This was the first time Oliana felt that there was a wall between them. She had lost the oasis and was left alone in this beautiful dazzling desert-mansion.

– – –

# Chapter 14

Mahealeani often thought of her daughter now so far away on the mainland. She did miss her—her lovely smile, soft touches, and childlike innocence. She knew that her only child was financially well off and that she would never ever have to worry about money - that she would have all the comforts that the world has to offer and Jonathan would be always with her.

"But is she really happy?" she would often ask herself.

Almost every time, her memories would hark back to Oliana's childhood and some of these reminiscences kept repeating themselves in her mind. She remembered when she entered the room and almost gasped as wraiths began moving toward her. Suddenly, they veered away and when she collected her senses, she realized that these were no wraiths, but only the shadows cast on the wall by someone moving about with sinuous grace.

"Who could it be?" she wondered as she stood on the stoop and watched the shadows play on the wall.

"Heavens! It is only little Oliana," she muttered to herself marveling at the same time at the style and charm of the movements of the six year old. It was as if her every movement signified a word, as if the child were possessed. Was she possessed by Pele, Goddess of the Volcano? The shadows seemed to emanate the mysticism and spirituality, the very attributes that had been credited to that powerful goddess.

As Mahealeani stood there in the relative darkness, she was unwilling to break the spell certain she knew that the silhouette of her daughter represented something more than just a child at play. Although Oliana was her only child, Mahealani well knew that most children sing before they speak and dance almost before they walk and that music is in the heart from the very beginning. Yet it was incredible, she thought, that one so young could make dance movements that seemed at once choreographed and innate. Mahealani knew at once that her daughter possessed something more than just a natural sense of rhythm and grace of movement. It was much more than that.

"Where did you learn to dance like that?" Mahealeani asked the child when the shadows on the wall stopped moving and she revealed her presence to her daughter.

"I don't know, mama. My feet just move. Like a dream."

If it was like a dream, it was as if it were Oliana's feet that were dreaming. It was spiritual, as if the hallowed dancers of ancient Hawaii had been reincarnated in this young girl. It was this that made Mahealani spends money she could ill afford on dance lessons.

Of course it was not the prohibitively expensive ballet classes that she sent Oliana to, but to a *halau*, classes where the Hawaiian *hula* dances were taught, where the hula was danced to the beat of the traditional percussion instruments like sharkskin drums, feather-decorated gourds, bamboo stamping tubes, split bamboo rattles, and stone castanets as well as to the modern guitar and ukulele. It was there that Oliana picked up the sacred chants of the *hula* and learned that the *hula* was the history book of a people without a written language and that the chants maintained the relationship between gods and mortals, heralding chiefs, celebrating sex and procreation, and venerating the subtleties of the world of nature—tumbling waterfalls, the moon and its many facets, the myriad mists and the rain of the islands.

The *halau* taught Oliana the mysteries of the time-honored *hula kahiko* with its percussion-driven poetic chants that honored the powerful gods of legend. It taught her the modern *hula 'auana*, the fluid and graceful dance that also came so naturally to her.

However, it was not just her ability to dance that surprised Mahealani. She was like a child of the forest. No, that wasn't quite right—she was like a princess of the forest.

Mahealani used to work in a souvenir shop in Hilo. As a teenager, Oliana would invariably spend her holidays with her. Mahealeani's mind would often travel over time and distance to that scene and in her mind's eye would recall everything as they were in those far off days. It was a charming place. Just behind the shop was a waterfall, formed by a clear stream that ran down a sinuous course through the dark green forest to form a deep green pool and then ran on, shallow and crystalline, past rocks to a sandy beach.

Tropical trees grew thickly and stood in frivolous elegance, all clad in trailing plants, around the pool and they were reflected in the green water in the light of the sun that played fitfully through the leaves on the sparkling water. Overhead, the myna birds made a great to do and made the scene complete. It was a place replete with tropical richness and there was a scent there that was all pervading. The water was fresh but not cold and it was just right for swimming. Oliana would spend most of her time cavorting around and splashing gaily in the water, diving, resting on the banks of the pool. She would wander for hours in the forest that was just behind the waterfall and soon knew every nook and cranny in that wonderful place. She would adorn herself with flowers and her budding young breasts would be covered with them. But she seemed oblivious to everything around her for she took no notice of anyone as she played about in that almost mystic place. When Mahealani looked at her, she had the queer feeling that she was invisible, for Oliana paid no heed to anything when she was there.

When Oliana stood there with the ever-present breeze from the ocean, it was as if she were a princess, a princess of the forest, at once regal and earthy, as if everything was waiting for the touch of her hands and feet, to spring to life. Mahealani looked beyond her and noted that the tide was well out, but had turned. Between her and the gentle ripple of white foam marking the water's edge there was an expanse of golden sand and as she gazed at the pounding surf beyond the coconut trees that crowded upon the coral shore, she wondered what strange thoughts wandered through Oliana's head.

The teachers at the *halau* told Mahealani that her daughter had a rare but natural grace and love for the *hula*. But they told her that a true teacher's job was not to teach, but to offer stimulation and ways in which the students can educate themselves. All that a teacher could do was wake up that person and make the person hungry.

"In the old days hula would have been Oliana's calling," one of the teachers told Mahealani. "You know how it was in those days."

Mahealani knew. It was like joining the priesthood or a nunnery and the initiation processes were very complicated.

"Yes and those *hula* dancers spent a lot of time to get initiated in the many processes."

"Today, it's a pastime, not a calling," Mahealani replied.

"The hula, expresses everything we see, feel, hear, smell, taste and touch," they told her. "But it's not about technique alone. It has to do with passion. Oliana has a rare but natural grace and love for the dancing and the passion for it."

"Yes, she is always dancing. Even when she talks, her hands move so gracefully."

"*Hula* choreography is not just about the movements of the hands. It embraces the feet as well as lyrical body motions reflecting nature and dynamic changes in the pursuit of perfection."

"I know that. I meant that she is naturally very graceful, and she's not aware of it most of the time. The point is, you can't see a painter or a writer or a musician if you just look at them, but you can see a dancer in a child if it has studied dance for even a year."

"That's true. But you don't dance with your hands; you dance with your feet. It's the feet that take you around, not your hands. That is why we insist that the dancers should keep the feet flat and teach them to sway into the steps through natural controlled hip movements so that they appear as if they are floating across the stage."

"I noticed that."

"The feet shouldn't skid, tap, or jerk. Dancing with the feet is one thing, but dancing with the heart is another. That's why although you can't see a painter or a writer or a musician if you just look at them, you can see a dancer in a child if they've studied dance for even a year."

Mahealani understood that, but was flummoxed when one of the teachers asked her if she had seen Oliana dance the *He Po Lani Makamae*, for she did not know what it was. That was not surprising, for *hula* choreography depends on one's tradition and this differs from island to island.

"It is a dance that wonders at the beauty of a newborn child seen in the light of the full moon," the teacher told her when she realized that Mahealani did not know of the dance and she had not seen Oliana dance it either.

She had once seen her perform that dance, but it was not those images that kept coming back, but those of the *Hivaiki hula*. Oblivious to her surroundings, Oliana danced impersonally, her eyes staring into space. At first she swayed delicately, her dark eyes fixed on the ground.

Then, as the dance progressed, she led the percussion instruments to an ever increasing tempo and rhythm until it seemed that her body was on fire. The bright yellow light shining off the glow of her perspiring golden brown skin added to the illusion. It was as if she were the Goddess Pele, rising from her fiery volcanic home.

"The physical language of the body is so much more powerful than words," Mahealeani told herself for the hundredth time.

Oliana danced out of herself. It made her larger, more beautiful, and more powerful. It was as if she was revealing her power—the power and glory on earth and telling one and all that it was hers for the taking. But it was not just athletic. Yes, one had to be athletic to be a dancer, but it took an artiste to be a dancer.

She danced on her toes with her knees and elbows spread out spread her legs excitingly in a display that was at once full of balletic grace. Slowly, she spread her arms allowing her movements to become ever more challenging. Then the drums slowed down. She closed her eyes and held her head back, her long hair hanging down, in a mass of night-black tresses. This was the dance that was at once the ballet of a woman in furious love with raw nature. Her partner seemingly awakened with her every movement danced on in perfect time to the percussion and then as the tempo picked up once more, his movements became more vigorous. The two dancers kept up the vigorous tempo like athletes of the Gods. Then, as the drums reached a fever pitch, Oliana's partner leapt high in the air and landed with perfect poise inches away from her. All at once, the drums stopped beating and in the dead silence that followed, Oliana moved away, her head bowed until at last she was lost in the shadows of the stage.

Then, like a dam breaking its walls, the crowd broke into thunderous applause. Mahealani woke up with a start and rubbed her eyes. How long she had lain there remembering the past, she wasn't sure. She had no idea. She sat up.

"Dance was always the language of her soul and she always revealed her love of herself in the freedom of her dance. But why do I keep dreaming of her so often these days and the very same dreams over and over again?" she asked aloud in the quietness of her room.

# Chapter 15

Sometimes, when Oliana was depressed about Jonathan's indifference toward her, or when she thought of Hawaii sadly, she made herself act as though nothing were wrong. She would tell herself firmly and aloud, "I have it all. I need nothing more." She would try to suppress her inner feelings as she knew that nobody would understand her situation, except perhaps Susan.

They were sitting on the balcony of Susan's little apartment near the university that day. Though she did not utter it loudly, Susan heard her and asked what she was worried about. "What is wrong, Oliana? Susan asked.

"Nothing. It's such a chore just to pass the day," Oliana moaned.

"Come on!" Susan said as she lay back in her deck chair and observed her through glasses. Susan was about the only true friend Oliana had made at university and they met regularly. For the past few months, Oliana had begun calling on her more frequently.

"I find myself changing. I'm no longer the person I was a few months ago."

"No one is. We change with each and every passing day," Susan said philosophically.

"Yes, I know we do, but that's not what I mean."

"What exactly is the problem?"

"I'm changing into someone I don't quite like. Look at me."

"Oh, no! You're still the lovely beautiful young woman who I met at college all those semesters ago. You are as passionate as always and you never let go of your heritage," Susan said affectionately.

"Outwardly perhaps. But deep down I feel so different. Maybe it is so superficial here—and it's perhaps because I cannot do the things I want to do."

"Like what?"

"Like surfing."

"Come on! You can always go off to California. Get Jonathan to take you on a holiday to the sunshine state."

"It's not quite the same. In Hawaii, I was free to do what I wanted. I could go surfing whenever I wanted." Oliana looked sad.

"Is that such a big deal, Oliana? Everything is meaningful even if it is sometimes beyond our understanding and there is the knowledge that there is a tomorrow." She paused for a moment then said "As for me, I have surfed. And I know what its like," Susan said philosophically.

"You've just surfed the way most tourists on the beach do. It's not quite the same. For us, surfing is a way of life, an experience in which you feel at one with the ocean and worship."

"Like your hula dance?"

"Not quite like that, but yes in a way that's true"

"But there's so much more to life than hula and surfing. Isn't there?"

"Perhaps, but these are my inner feelings, I want to glide through the river, look at the stars as long as I want, that endless sky- the stars tell me the story as they have witnessed the saga of many generations of many traits. I miss the chants and the tradition of my land and the mighty volcano," Oliana said softly and looked away on the sky as she wiped her eyes.

Susan asked firmly, "Please tell me Oliana what else is wrong. It seems that something more is wrong and you are not telling me." Susan realized something else also was bothering Oliana and it was not only the surfing or the quest for freedom.

"My in-laws always expect so much from me but I don't want to let them down. I don't want to hurt them, and especially lately, Jonathan—lately his attitude, he is always wrapped up in his own thoughts, and work. He does not tell me what is going on in his mind. I get so confused— These are the matters that I cannot ignore sometime. I do not know what to do."

"Life can be found only in the present. The past is gone and the future is yet to be. Have you thought about that, Oliana? I know you are so young and you have to grow up so fast. It is so sad that at your age you would only be enjoying life, - laughing, dancing, joking but now you have to deal with serious matters. " Susan tried to console her.

"I do, but I have so many conflicting feelings—sometimes I think of Hawaii, the hula, my spiritual existence and then the next moment I think of Jonathan, my love, my life. Maybe I should leave Houston for a while, go somewhere to sort out my contradictory feelings.

"You are not going to do any such thing. Why don't the two of you go to Hawaii for a while?"

"I suppose so, but that will depend more on him than on me."

"Where is Jonathan, by the way?"

"He's working late again tonight"

"Do you love him, Oliana?"

"He is the entire world to me. I adore him, but now I'm torn between that love for him and what I feel compelled to do. I want to be alone. I cannot allow myself to be imprisoned by these contradictory feelings. Maybe I have to keep my solitude for a while" she said softly as if she was speaking to herself.

"Don't walk out on him. Talk to him when he returns." Susan was concerned when Oliana told her about her heartbreaking observations of Jonathan's indifferent attitude toward her lately.

Oliana nodded her head. What was the remedy to love, but more love, she wondered. She was tired and wondered whether she would have the energy she needed to talk to Jonathan when he returned. Lately Jonathan was so absorbed by his own feeling in his own world that he forgot to pay any attention to Oliana. "Don't you see, Jonathan, your own island flower, as you say always lovingly, is drying"—Oliana wanted to agitate him and say that to him.

And that moment, Oliana could not help thinking of the excitement of the days when he had first come to Hawaii. The ecstasy of their meetings, the beauty and brilliance that they saw in even the most mundane objects, laughter over nothing and the sensation that there was nobody in the whole wide world but the two of them. She had thought that they had discovered the joy of each other. Perhaps they had, but she was not so certain now.

Her thoughts came back to the present. "What am I going to do? She asked again. Susan wiped the rest of the tears like morning dews from her sad stricken lovely face and hugged her for a moment. "Maybe, Oliana, you are imagining that," she said doubtfully. Perhaps some solution would come to her when the time would really come.

— — —

When Oliana returned from Susan's apartment, she saw Jonathan was going through some papers. Oliana sat down beside him and said lovingly, "hi." He did not even look or respond. He was too busy with his work. Oliana remembered the times when he would read for a while, then he would stop and the two of them would kiss passionately for hours. She remembered those days when he asked her what she wanted out of life and how she had told him of some of her dreams and her hopes for the future. He would listen intently and promise to make it all happen, and he said it in such a way that she would actually believe him. She knew now, however, those feelings were distant.

She could sense that old feeling welling within her, that feeling of self-doubt, that unwillingness to bring it out in the open, that reluctance to look into his eyes and ask what's going on. Jonathan could not see the look of pain in her eyes. She had observed that he had become quiet and withdrawn for some time now, and preferred to think that it may be a passing phase and had hoped that he would get over it soon. She had made quite a few attempts to bring him around. When Jonathan looked at her finally, she thought she had to bring it up. When she opened her mouth to speak, she found to her surprise that she was calm and collected.

"I can't stay here anymore, Jonathan," she said without any preamble. Jonathan stared at her, his mouth half open as this was a bolt from the blue, something he never expected.

"I don't know what you mean?" he sputtered.

"I feel my world closing in on me."

"Stop talking in riddles," he said.

"I'm not talking in riddles. I can't stay here anymore. I am going away. I need to be back home."

"This is your home, my love," he reminded her.

"No. No matter how hard I try, and I have, I've not been able to think of it that way, Jonathan," she said sadly, her head drooping on her shoulders. "Jonathan, my love for you is forever but you are putting a wall between us. Now you are far away and wrapped up in your own world. Jonathan, you do not pay any attention to me. We hardly go out any more or make love."

"That's not true. When did I do that?" he denied. Oliana knew there no point in arguing. Oliana thoughts of the ocean and the waves of Hawaii—many times the waves come to shore to hug passionately but had to leave the shore in vain to go back to the ocean.

Jonathan watched her mood to keep control as usual. Her eyes were shut and she did not want to show what was going on in her mind. It had never been like this, and when she looked at him, he felt tightness in his stomach.

When he finally spoke, his voice was steady, but there was pain in it and Oliana could sense it. "How can you say that? Everyone especially I have done everything possible to make you feel at home and now Jason has admitted to rehab, you have nothing to worry about." He said again.

"Made me feel at home, yes, but that's not what I am worried about now. Your indifference…" She could not finish. Her tone guarded but quiet, for she did not want to hurt him more. She went to the bathroom and broke into tears silently.

Why it happened, she would never know, but she had the feeling that this was when the chasm began to close for them. For a fleeting moment, though, a tiny wisp of time that hung in the air, she wondered if she fell in love with him again at this moment.

It was Jonathan who finally broke the leaden silence. "I've always wanted what's best for our happiness," he said simply when she returned. Afterwards, Oliana tried to remember the last time they had talked like this.

They rarely argued and it was always one of open discussion, a lot of give and take. She tried to explain that she needed to be closer to her people, her culture and yet also to him, if he let her. It had not seemed to make a difference before, but it did now as Oliana could sense that Jonathan was aloof and unapproachable recently.

"I know you have. And I love you for it," Oliana replied sadly. At that moment Jonathan wanted to touch her, to take her in his arms and kiss her, but he didn't. He vaguely wondered whether things would be better if they made love that night, but then realized that it was not the solution for the problem at hand.

As for Oliana, the demon of choice confronted her. It teased and challenged her. She could not figure it out anymore definitely. If it were between love and hate, she could have handled it. But it wasn't. It was between her deep love for Jonathan and a clash of cultures and now also Jonathan's unapproachable attitude towards life. How one could handle that, she did not know. She tried to find an answer in his eyes but there was nothing. And so she let the matter drop and did not bring it up again.

---

Later that night, Jonathan went back to the office. He had a lot of doubts about the dealings and wheeling of the company. After reaching Foster Holdings, he asked security to open the door of his father's office. The door was locked with a secret code that Jonathan did not know. After pushing the code button, the security man let him enter the office.

Jonathan went through the files in the drawers and computers to see for himself if what he was suspected were true. He was truly shocked. He had some doubt and gut feelings that there were a few minor things wrong. But the enormity, the atrocity, and the extent of violations and corruptions he witnessed on the page after page were beyond his imagination. He was disoriented and puzzled.

After coming back from the office, Jonathan wanted to go back to sleep so that he could think fresh in the morning but another sleepless night was due for Jonathan. All the complicated thoughts were crushing his tangled mind. He thought of his father and then his mother. His father's corrupted nature, his addiction for money, and greed to possess it in any way without any moral distressed him. Occasionally he would try to intervene and even confront him but it would not deter him from what he was determined to do. Then he thought of his beloved mother who valued all the lavishness life had to offer and the affluent, sumptuous lifestyle she adored. With a stroke of SEC who is sleeping in the job and who failed to prosecute at this moment, or looked the other way, temporarily, would crumble into pieces like a glass menagerie. This very thought chilled Jonathan's body temporarily. It was absolutely tortuous for Jonathan. At the same time, he was miserable because he was unable to approach with the information. He had a prior knowledge and had to tell the authority.

Later that night Jonathan had trouble falling asleep. The next morning he had to give serious thought again to this matter as it needed a final decision and solution.

"To live in it with its luxury, pretending knowing nothing, and depriving others what are lawfully theirs, is absolutely impossible and immoral." He repeated those words many times. Letting his father know that he would not be able to stay with the company would make his father absolutely furious - he knew that as well. But before he could undertake the final decision, he wanted some advice from his best friend OC. He wanted to lift up this heavy burdened venture from his mind. He could not carry this horrific situation alone any more. The next morning OC received a phone call from Jonathan urging him to have lunch with him that day. OC was overwhelmed and accepted the invitation -whenever he could help Jonathan out.

"Everyone's tense at the office these days." Jonathan did not know how to break the news to OC.

"Why?"

"I guess you've been away and don't know many things about my father's company. Though I've never been comfortable with the way my father operates his business, I did know now exactly what he does. I found out all the corrupt deals he made with other companies - the accounting fraud and cheating the shareholders. Oh my god, I cannot bear any more. One of these days my fear is, it looks, as if the long arm of the law is about to catch up with him. The saddest thing is that confrontation with him did not help. There's no one I can talk to. You are my best friend whom I can trust." He repeated, "I am so lucky to have you as a friend." He paused for a moment then said,

"If it was not my dad, it would have been so easy for me, but it is not the case. I couldn't stay here anymore. I could not stand this deception, this immoral act. I wish I could take my Oliana and leave.

This is so sad that it has to be this way. Now do you realize why I feel so lost and worried? What do I do now? I want your advice desperately in this matter."

Realizing the agony Jonathan was going through OC replied, "If you want my advice I think you are right about it. You tried your best to deter your father by confronting but it did not work. You should leave the company and when the time comes you give a hand to your father and law enforcement, Jonathan."

OC's words preyed on his mind. The more he dwelt on it, the clearer it became. He shook hands with OC and said, "Thanks for your support, my friend. I will never forget your help. I needed that." OC smiled and answered, "No problem, it was my pleasure to help you out."

"Yes, I will call my father now to tell him that I am going to leave the company. I know he will be mad but he left me without any choice. Oliana was right." Moments later Jonathan called his father at work after gathering all his strength.

"Dad, I have decided that I will not go back to the company any more. I am leaving the company. You will definitely find a suitable person in my place." On the other end of the phone he could hear the thunder rolling over the dark sky. Jonathan could not hear what his father was saying to him but he could guess. He became frozen for a while- the world was going around him as usual in its own rhythm, only Jonathan was standing still. Finally, he got off the phone and sat still for a while. Though the harsh treatment over the phone by his father and his own anguish over this matter left him with a trace of melancholy and sadness, he was jubilant that he would no longer be a part of that corrupt institution.

This inner turmoil and complicated self questioning made him aware that it was coming from his belief in moral values for deeper and broader social agenda like fighting poverty and specifically economic injustice to the poor. His philosophy was that rich people have more responsibility to engage in to end poverty and hunger but they are going away from that philosophy and becoming greedy and self-serving. Jonathan was always inspired by universal morality that is based on absolute standard

*In Pursuit of Love, Spirituality and Happiness*

and cultural morality that is based on culture. Jonathan knew that in the ancient days, Romans enjoyed the death of a gladiator who was killed by the lion. It was the culture of that time. Though it was questionable to others, this kind of moral value was governed by culture. There were many things that do not meet the absolute standard like same-sex unions, arranged marriage, dress code for westerner or middle easterner, death by hanging. Jonathan often wondered about cultural morality that has a different set of value. But this time he was making an assessment about universal morality and his own consciousness.

---------

In modern days, the gospel of Americanism was rooted in justice, freedom, and liberty combined with romanticism for spiritual practice and religious freedom, as OC would say, "spiritual but not overly religious." Jonathan had seen the effect and consequences with his father's experimentation in religion. He did read a report published by Pew Forum that mainline Protestant churches are in decline, non-denominational churches are gaining –it also provided a deeper look behind those trends. Jonathan examined his own belief after he left the job. "Right now, there is a dropping on confidence in organized religion, especially in the traditional religious forms." Jonathan was influenced by the appeal of John Paul II and Dalai Lama. This was a different ideology than his father's dogmas laid down by him. Jonathan viewed this new ideology and spiritualism, coming from multiculturalism and taking roots in his American life, and would be free of ritualistic approaches and adopt his own spiritualistic value. Buddhism was gaining popularity in here. Jonathan was touched by the philosophy of Buddhism as well like his other friends in America. He knew most of his American friends and acquaintances were craving new and dynamic insight of spiritual aspects. He was also no longer satisfied with the authoritative God where there were no spiritual connections. He had adopted a secondary principle like Buddhism which was giving him some peace in his mind what he was craving for now-a-days. He read many books on Buddhist philosophy and contacted and listened to many monks on these subjects. These second vision gave him some inner peace but Jonathan was agitated with this thought as he had so many questions about Christianity and was trying to come to resolve his confusion in his mind.

He vividly remembered the long conversation he had with OC a few days ago. "Do you believe suffering is punishment for sin as the Prophets say?" Jonathan asked.

OC replied, "That's not true. If you say that's true then why do children suffer from cancer, malnutrition, etc. They do not commit any sin. People pollute the environment by being greedy. They inflict harms on others by fighting and being power hungry. You can see the evidence of holocaust in Bosnia, Sudan, Kenya and Rwanda to name a few. God could not come down to earth to make it right. The appearance of God on earth would be with such enormous energy and power it would demolish the whole world. But from time to time great souls like Jesus (Son, distinguished from Father), Gandhi, civil rights leader Martin Luther King, Ram, Dalai lama, collectively and individually good people solve the problem and punish those who inflict harm. You know an individual who impose harm to others gets punished by our justice system and is criticized through public opinion. Another thing is that we think nature's fury is God's punishment. That is not true either because nature is bound by its own rules to produce storm or natural disaster. I believe prayer helps and If you pray hard God will help you."

Jonathan was satisfied with the explanation. He had another question and asked, "Is the suffering a test from God?"

OC smiled and then looked at his friend. He saw Jonathan had not combed his hair, his shirt was not buttoned properly, and his face was smeared with tension. He understood the dilemma and said, "Well, the book of Job said that. Remember when we read the Hebrew Bible and the New Testament and the story of Joseph? In this case, Joseph absolutely dedicated himself to God with his free will. God tested him to see if his faith was absolute and strong and whether he could control himself from all the allure around him and withstand any despair like losing his children (how horrendous that was). then only he can go to him. God can also purify the person like gold by letting him suffering, if that person voluntarily wants to dedicate his life to him. As you know, God does not grant us any material things but gives us non-material things like strength, wisdom, consciousness, knowledge, love, intelligence, humor, and talent. We make the choice with our free will and subsequent consequences follow. By now I would have been a billionaire if God listened to my prayer."

Jonathan and OC laughed together. Later Jonathan said in a doubtful voice, "It seems like the Bible is contradictory."

"It is not at all. It is all in the right interpretation. We could establish a spiritual connection only if we know the right interpretation of the Bible and of course, it has to be interpreted on a human level. Originally, in the history of human beings, everything was mysterious - storm, fire, rain everything was explained as a divine intervention and early Christianity was not an exception. The Bible emphasized that everybody should act like a saint and lots of restriction were enforced. Individuality was denied. Too many rituals were observed. A ritualistic approach is only good to prepare the atmosphere and the mind but it stops there. It does not establish any spiritual connection to God, and if you impose lots of restrictions in your mind you would not be free. You know my grandfather said the Hindu religion has fewer restrictions, and it deals with the human condition. We can learn from each other. I have lots of respect for my grandfather who worships Kali, the protector of good and the destroyer of evil. The Buddhist religion enlightens the world and you, since you took it as a secondary belief system. And for me, no matter how much influence I have from my grand father and my secondary faith, but when I close my eyes to pray, I see Jesus' face and that makes my heart cry. The Bible is wonderful but it needs a new interpretation on the human level. It needs to deal with the human condition as we are just ordinary human beings. We are not all saints who need very high standard of value."

Jonathan was very interested and was trying to understand his own confusion, "I do not understand. What do you mean?"

OC said, "I do not know if you have seen that movie where in the Catholic church the nuns tried to convince the girls who were in their dormitory that they should not pay any attention to the outer world. One of the girls was playing a popular Beatles' songs and she was punished heavily. We are all part of the world and not out of the world. Of course, people who hold religious positions and govern by higher theology should have a much higher standard than ordinary people. Otherwise, they will be like us, ordinary people. We do not understand that religion has two facets –first is the relationship with our God and other is the relationship with other humans. Some times we mixed up two facets of religion. I think the Bible and churches can play a significant role in our lives. We need love, assurance, and a pat on the back from God and a direction of how to lead our daily lives. We need to respect ourselves and others and not to hurt others."

Jonathan said sadly, "I feel so guilty that I haven't gone to church for months but years ago when I used to go, I felt so peaceful. With so much commotion in the office, colleagues and my parents and aggravation in day to day life I needed my church but something has changed in recent days. "

OC replied, "It is the same with me. Of course, I know in recent years some white Churches have had many sexual scandals and Some black churches substitute hatred. I don't think that is churches' role. Spiritual leaders should not act as activists or political leaders who debate in the public forum to get justice. Spiritual leaders should work behind the scenes with a non-violent approach. When we go to church, our mind should fill up with joy and our mind will heal. We should keep our faith as it is the great understanding of our own existence and there lies the deep root between us. Without spirituality, we would not know ourselves. There is greatness in the world and we touch the greatness through spirituality. " They both agreed and submerged into profound thoughts since they both adopted a secondary belief system with the primary one.

# Chapter 16

Oliana had left early in the morning without saying anything to Jonathan. So it was only when Jonathan returned home and called her name a few times then he realized she was gone. The staff did not remember her driving out in the Audi that Jonathan had given her on her last birthday. The garage was not connected to the mansion, and no one had seen her get into the car or knew if she'd taken a suitcase with her.

Jonathan was very eager to tell Oliana the news about his leaving the company and the undivided attention he could give her now. Jonathan indulged himself in the fantasy of those sweet thoughts and waited for her return so that he would give her the exciting news.

A few hours passed. This had never happened before. Oliana always let Jonathan know where she was. With horrible disappointment Jonathan realized and suspected now that maybe she had gone home or left him. She had been uneasy, he knew, for the past few weeks, and although he did not know the depth of her feelings, he had some idea of her state of mind. He had thought that it would blow over.

When she left, Jonathan did not understand the real reason, though just the week before she had hinted to Jonathan that she might want to visit her parents. "It's just for a couple of weeks. I need a break."

Jonathan had not said anything at first. He had always had a feeling that someday something would happen and he and Oliana would be separated. He could not understand why this feeling would occupy him sometimes. Maybe the deep love within him created this separation anxiety disorder.

This, however, was so unlike her. So different from the gentle beauty he had grown to love so well. She had wanted to go home and that he could well understand. What he could not fathom was her leaving without even saying "good bye."

In the years that they had been together she had become everything to he wanted. He knew he should spend more time with her. He had vowed to do that when he got married, but the business limited his hours and all the corrupt dealings in the company made it even more impossible. Oliana had always seemed to understand. But on that occasion he had not said anything much, his face would freeze up as he felt guilty about it. He told her "I wish I could give you what you want. The trouble is that I could not at this moment. I know that there's a part of me at this moment that is closed off from you and my mind is somewhere else. .but I would resolve this matter pretty soon. You will see. We will be together again. "

The words were spoken with such sincerity that she knew he wasn't just saying it. He truly believed in what he said and for that reason it meant much more to her than she expected. But could she really rely on it or wait any longer for his attention or love – so many days had passed in vain?

Thoughts of the days when he had come to Hawaii came back to her. As she stared at him, she noticed how he had changed since then. Although there were the signs of strain and he still looked boyish and handsome and for the thousandth time she asked herself if she really should leave. Should she give herself some more time to make a go of their marriage? No, it would not work out, not in Houston, until Jonathan comes out from the cocoon, she thought.

Never again would she sit alone in their suite of rooms in the Foster mansion waiting for Jonathan to come home. Never again would she indulge in fantasies. That was why nothing quite dampened her resolve. She knew there was no way she could tell him what she planned to do as she would not be able to bear the look on his face if she told him that she would not be coming back.

The inspiration to return to Hawaii was haunting her now. More and more she was hearing the call of the volcano goddess from the far away land; the enchanted drum beats were becoming irresistible to her senses. As Jonathan's deep attention to her every day's need was evaporating she was becoming restless and every single day her deep commotion of spiritual exploration with nature was becoming a reality.

– – –

The flights from Houston to Los Angeles and from there to Honolulu were long, but uneventful. She switched off her cell phone as soon as she left the mansion so that she would not have to answer anyone. There had been a few occasions when the phone had not worked and she hoped that Jonathan would assume that was the case, until it was too late. She traveled all the way to Honolulu without speaking to anyone except the flight attendants and those manning the check in counters. In Honolulu, she caught a flight to Hilo and exited the airport as fast as she could and caught a taxi to go to volcanic park.

The sky was in reddish color. It seemed like Mother Nature took some red dye in her hand and in playful nature she threw it all over the sky. As Oliana crossed the threshold of volcanic park, it came to life. From one of the mountains, hot glowing lava started to flow and the other mountain started to shoot up the fire balls as high as it could reach. Oliana bowed down on her knees and apologized for being disobedient and far away, and then she got up and in a very slow motion with extended arms followed the slight gesture of dance. She remembered a quotation Susan used to repeat to her. "If the sight of the blue skies fills you with joy, if a blade of grass springing up in the fields has power to move you, if the simple things of nature have a message that you understand, rejoice, for your soul is alive..."

She had not told her mother anything about her plans to come. When the taxi drew up before her mother's house, there was no one at home. She let herself in with the key, which she had not given back to her mother. It was one of the few things that she had kept as a reminder that her home was on the Hawaiian Islands. It was an important link to the past that she had left behind and she did not want to relinquish it.

The little house was exactly as it had been when she left for Houston. It was not anywhere as opulent or even as comfortable as the Foster mansion in Houston, but it was good to be back home. This was where she was at her happiest, she told herself as she slumped into the sofa.

---

Jonathan called the airlines and learned that Oliana had caught a flight to Los Angeles where she had changed flights and caught one to Hawaii. He tried to get her on her mobile phone, but knew after a few attempts that she had switched it off.

"She'll come back," he told himself as he sat down wearily in an armchair.

He thought of calling Oliana's mother, but did not want to make her worry as he was not absolutely sure that Oliana was there. So he could do nothing but wait and he did, confident that Oliana would call him back soon.

However, the next day when Jonathan did not hear from her he became very frustrated. He could not concentrate on anything. He thought how helplessly unhappy he was and knew that it was because of the loss of her presence, which he had taken for granted, that caused it. He tried to console himself with the thought that even the deepest love required renewal by intervals of absence and that she would come back soon. But as the day passed he began to find that absence is to love what wind is to fire; It was as if his love for Oliana had been rekindled to burn with a greater flame. He only realized it now as Oliana was not there anymore.

He remembered reading somewhere that a man can be himself only so long as he is alone and that if he did not love solitude, he would not love freedom. But he did not want to be alone, he did not want freedom; he just wanted to be with Oliana. What was the purpose of life without her—without her to share the beauty of the stars, to laugh with, to touch and to hold? Nothing was meaningful anymore. Everything was hollow and empty to Jonathan now.

These thoughts preyed on his mind and the more he dwelled on them, the clearer it became. "If she would not come to me, I would go to her." Without her, life was becoming unbearable to Jonathan. He blamed himself for not being responsive and caring.

"Oliana, my sweet island flower, come back. Don't you see I cannot exist without you," he said many times, as if, he was hoping hearing his voice she would not be able to resist.

# Chapter 17

Jonathan became increasingly frustrated the next day when he did not hear anything from her. He could not contemplate on anything. He understood how miserable he was without Oliana. He had taken for granted that Oliana would stay with him forever. He tried to console himself with the thought that even the deepest love required renewal by intervals of absence, but that did not provide any comfort to his grief. As the day passed, he became more and more depressed. A despondent, melancholic feeling was setting in. He remembered how he had been stung both by beauty and desire when he had first seen Oliana, how his heart had started pounding and he had felt dizzy. He could almost visualize her on a surfboard with her long hair streaming behind her in the wind and see her swaying to the languorous strains of a Hawaiian melody as she surfed. He could not wait any longer and, in desperation, he called Susan on the cell phone. "Hello, Susan, do you have any information about Oliana. She left Houston."

Susan was not surprised. She had a premonition that one of these days Oliana would leave Houston. She replied in a calm voice, "She did not call me either, but I tried to call her on her cell phone and there is no response. I am sure she will call back soon. By the way, one more thing, I am going back to New York. If you see her, please tell her that and also tell her that I miss her everyday and give my love."

Jonathan was greatly disappointed with Susan's answer. Then he said sadly, "I know she will love to hear that. I know how she feels about you. I will tell her that when I see her." Jonathan was calling from the terrace - the terrace that led out of their suite of rooms was where Oliana and he would spend those evenings closely in love when they stayed in. It was there that he felt at his happiest when she was there and loneliest after she left. He could almost smell the gardenia perfume that she invariably wore and feel her presence by his side. He often would hear Oliana's sweet laughter in the air. He sometimes looked at the endless sky, he saw the clouds are forming like a beautiful lady—Is it my sweet Oliana?

– – –

Oliana had left with just a small valise and her engagement ring. Practically all the lovely designer clothes that Jonathan and his mother had bought her were left behind in the closet as was all the diamond and gold jewelry, including the diamond studded choker set in white gold and the diamond earrings that were his first presents to her. The room, indeed, was full of the things that were hers and seeing them only added to his misery. He touched each one, one by one—every touch brought the thrill of the past memory and at the same time unbearable pain to his vein. That was the only existence of Oliana he could feel at this moment.

Jonathan had taken quite a few digital photographs, but had never gotten around to putting them together into any order or even selecting the good ones. They were all stored on his laptop. They were often at hand in the office and Jonathan would go over each picture with scenes from their days together at different seasons at different hours of the day. These were the pictures that, every so often, kept him breathing when he wanted to recall the cool morning breezes of their days together. That varied from location to location, from mountains to deserts. They were the only reminders that there was, somewhere, a cold blue sea, spread like a satin sheet early in the morning, the feel of wet sand under their feet, as they ran along the shoreline, cutting through the gentle waves that swept in and out.

His thoughts wandered back to Hawaii….the water gently lapping between his toes, washing away the sand…a soft, cool breeze slithering across his chest, caressing, giving him goose bumps where his skin was wet. As he felt each gentle sweep of the sea lap at his feet, he let it suck a piece of the frustration that was welling up inside him and he could feel the heat inside him cooling off bit by bit by Oliana's melodious touch.

"Why are these joyful moments turned into painful memories?" he wondered with anguish, sorrow, and distress. Although Jonathan had a very good and easygoing relationship with his mother, he knew he could not talk to her about this problem since she was out of town. She was always busy with her clubs and charity works, traveling to Paris and London's most prestigious fashion shows with sparkling diamonds, designer gowns, and the luncheon dates with the governor's and corporate wives. On the other hand, there was no question of discussing this problem with his father—he could never ever bring himself to do that. In any case, he was far too caught up in his own world of stocks, bonds, and corporate domain. Undeniably, Jonathan's misery had little value to him. Everything could be replaced in his view and now it would be even more difficult as he had left the corporation - It was out of the question now.

Jonathan tried to cope with it himself, trying to understand what his life could mean. Sometimes, there was a mild adrenaline rush associated with it, a feeling of being alive but most of the time he didn't care much, one way or another.

Often he was too tired to keep the anguish at bay, and his demons visited him, trying to invade the emptiness inside. He went down to his boat and took it out to some cove down Galveston where he and Oliana used to go. He would stare for hours on end at the horizon where the water and sky merged, finding some kind of peace in the serenity of the scene for a while but that was not sufficient for him.

OC had just returned from India. It was a great relief for Jonathan. It would be easy to talk to his old friend about Oliana and his love for her. He wanted to talk to him very much about what he now felt, and it was the time he was waiting for. He called OC and said sadly, "How are you OC? A horrible thing has happened to me. Oliana has gone. She left me. I've felt numb and disrupted ever since. I need Oliana desperately. I need her to share the beauty of the stars. I need her to be by my side—to laugh with, to touch and to hold. You can understand that, can't you OC?"

OC sensed the devastating hurt that crushed Jonathan's mind. "Yes. I can imagine, although I must confess that I have not been in love with anyone as deeply as you have with Oliana and although I can empathize with you, it may not be quite the same intensity of feeling I would have but I can picture what you are going through, Jonathan."

"I feel her presence all the time, and I see her everywhere. I see her in the clouds. I see them taking her form. I see her movements as they drift along in the sky. In my bedroom I can smell her fragrance everywhere," he said distractedly.

"I can imagine that, Jonathan. That kind of loneliness is experienced only when one is in love and separated. It is said that your heart withers when it does not answer another heart and your mind shrinks away when it hears only the echoes of our own thoughts and finds no other inspiration." OC tried to explain logically knowing that nothing would bring comfort to Jonathan until Oliana called him back.

"This is my fault. I did let her go. I did not pay any attention to her lately, and why do I feel so alone, OC?" Jonathan asked desperately.

"When you have love in your life, it compensates for many of the things you lack, but when that's not there, no matter what else is there, it is not quite enough. That is why you feel the pain of being alone so much. Go to Hawaii and try to get her back." OC tried to offer consolation to Jonathan. How long could Jonathan bear this tension, this emotional imbalance, this isolation—OC thought to himself.

"I suggest you to go to Hawaii, meet her, and talk to her. Find out what she wants." OC said philosophically again since he was exposed to many devout thoughts. Jonathan felt some relief after the conversation with OC.

"She is my life, OC, and I want to spend the rest of my life with her," Jonathan paused for a moment then he said,

"No matter what- without her I can't function. This huge empire means nothing to me. I have success defined by money, power, title, high-powered connection, but it means nothing at all. Without her, I cannot go on with my life. I will go to Hawaii whether she wants me or not." Then Jonathan placed his hands on OC's shoulder and said after taking a deep breath, "I am going to miss you tremendously. You are always there for me when I needed you the most. You always cheer me up whenever I am down. You always give me the best advice, which comes from the bottom of your precious heart. Our friendship will remain forever. Our lives may be destined in different directions but our friendship will always be strong enough to overcome that. It makes me sad inside, thinking that I have to leave everything in Houston, especially you, my friend. But I would never be happy without Oliana. You know how I feel about Oliana, her sweet smile takes my grief away. Without her everything in Houston is meaningless. So come and visit me there."

OC smiled at the thoughts but felt sad as he realized that soon Jonathan would leave for Hawaii to join with Oliana.

There was no one here OC felt so close to. Saying "good bye" would be terribly hard. With whom was he going to play golf or tennis or see the car show or sometimes even movies? All those memories came rushing back to him – the laughter, small stupid fights over nothing and then made it up and all those personal intimate secrets what you cannot tell any other person except your best friend. How he would cope with those; OC did not know. But despite his personal loss, he always knew that Jonathan's place was with Oliana. Sitting in Houston alone he would always imagine that Jonathan was doing well in a far away land and their friendship would never be lost.

# Chapter 18

Oliana vaguely remembered her mother coming to the table and sitting opposite her. She didn't ask too many questions about the reason for her coming. It was almost as if she had expected her to turn up unannounced. Oliana was glad that there were only few questions, for she was not really sure what she wanted to do in Hawaii. Nor was she prepared to answer questions about Jonathan and her relationship, for she had not really formulated them in her mind. Oliana's mother understood that looking at Oliana's distressed face.

"Something wrong? Are you okay?" she asked when she had caught her daughter's eye. "You look tired."

"No. Nothing. I'm fine," she replied. But though she denied it, Oliana could not help thinking about Jonathan all this time. Tear droplets started to form in her beautiful eyes. She missed Jonathan so much. Her tears said everything she could not express in words to her mother. Mahealeani took Oliana's face and pressed it on her chest. Mahealeani knew it was just a temporary separation. Oliana's love would win over. Mother and daughter cried together.

---

The letter was delivered and lay in the salver in the mantel piece in the suites. Jonathan was planning to go to Hawaii and making all the arrangements for the trip like arranging the limo and packing his suitcase. When he returned home from saying a heartrending "good bye" to OC, he didn't notice anything but reached out for the letter because of its lingering fragrance of gardenia that he had grown to associate with Oliana. He was overjoyed and after flipping it over in his hand, tore it open with trembling delight. He read the letter anxiously.

*My Darling, My Sweetheart,*

*I know I have been very unkind to leave you without a word.*

*My darling, I had to get away. The urge was too strong and I could not have left had I looked into your eyes when I said goodbye. I would have wavered, I know. I love you, Jonathan, and I always will and I can't bear to hurt you. I try to think what it's like for you, how you try to keep going day after day.*

*You are my best friend and my husband. I don't know which I enjoy most, but I treasure both and our life together, which has been simply wonderful. I think a lot about it now particularly when I close my eyes.*

*I hope that someday you may understand why I did what I did.*

*One more thing, I have been chosen to dance at the Polynesian cultural program a week from today.*

*Missing you with every pore of my being.*

*Yours forever,*

*Oliana*

Jonathan read the letter over and over again, trying to make out exactly what Oliana was trying to say. Yes, she missed him—that was so wonderful, most wonderful! His sweet Oliana loved him with every pore of being. This very word was repeated by him many times. Finally he had to figure it out if she really wanted him there with her. Was it an invitation to her debut on the Horizon stage?

These questions kept pounding him with an insistence that carried on well into that evening and throughout the night. He hardly slept and woke up bleary eyed. Oliana would want that or not, Jonathan's mind was set - to love her more- that irresistible feeling of touching her – kissing her the way he did when they first met – that heavenly encounter of love overwhelmed his mind. She was the one who excited his fancy and fantasy.

– – –

For the last time before leaving Houston, Jonathan went to say good bye to his boat and then to the mansion where he grew up – all the memories of childhood, adulthood came rushing back to him. Momentarily, he felt sad. But then he thought about Oliana - her loving nature, her spiritual dimension, her observing beauty in every little thing, her kindness that attracted him from the beginning in their romance. How could he wait any longer? He was getting restless.

As the flight swung over the azure blue water and began its descent to Honolulu, Jonathan's mind harked back to his very first trip to Hawaii. The memories came flooding back and he dwelled for a long while on how his life had changed since that visit.

He decided to check in at the Sheraton Royal Hawaiian Hotel, the very same hotel he had stayed at on his first visit. The only difference on this occasion was that he felt alone without Oliana and never thought how his destiny would bring him back again in this way with loneliness.

After a quick shower and a light lunch he set, out to the Polynesian Cultural Center, which he knew was at Laie, on the North Shore of the island. He asked the driver to take the more scenic route over the

Koolau mountains, and he sat back to enjoy the scenery and reminisce about Hawaii and falling in love with Oliana for the first time.

Even before he set out, he knew that he would be very early, but having reached Honolulu, he just couldn't sit around in his hotel until evening waiting for the program to start. He had to get to the venue even if he would not be able to see Oliana until the program was over.

Spread over 42 dazzling, tropical acres, the center represented practically all of Polynesia in one place. There were seven villages each representing a different part of Polynesia—Tonga, Tahiti, the Marquesas, Fiji, New Zealand, Samoa, and Hawaii. And it was really fascinating for each village re-enacted life as it was before the Europeans came and provided a flavor of Polynesia's cultural milieu.

He went around the center and tried to learn of the deep commitment that hula students put into their art, the heritage of the hula implements and instruments and gained a greater insight into Hawaiian culture. He watched women crafting leaves and flowers into beautiful Hawaiian lei and other useful items and then tried his hand at *ulu maika* a form of bowling devised by the Hawaiians.

He saw the *Hale Ali'i*, the chief's house that dominated the village by its size and height and the *Hale Papa'a*, where the chief stored his valuable possessions. Next door to that was the *Hale Pahu* where the drums and other sacred *hula* implements were stored. After going to the *Hale Ulana*, where the women demonstrate their handicraft skills, he went down to the food court where a great spread had been laid out. On the dot of five, the festivities for the Ali'I Luau began with a fresh flower *lei* greeting and the ceremonial lifting of the pig from the steaming rocks of the *imu*, the traditional Hawaiian underground oven. Jonathan knew that the *lu'au* was originally a lavish feast to honor royalty or foreign dignitaries.

Although there were no royalty or foreign dignitaries around, the spread that he saw at the center must have been as good as any *luau* ever. It was spectacularly authentic Hawaiian cuisine, he knew, and it was a delight to the eye—from *teriyaki* chicken and *lomi lomi* salmon, to a generous salad bar, chicken long rice, fresh fish, sweet potatoes, native fresh fruits, taro rolls, traditional desserts and, of course, poi. There was also the mouth watering *kalua* pork sliced from the pig that had just been taken out of the *imu*. It was an experience that he knew his heart and his palate would not forget for a long time. There were lots of tourists from mainland America, Japan, and Europe and for them American authentic cuisine was available too.

He did not know when Oliana would make her appearance on stage and he had learned to his dismay that there would be about 40 dancers in all. Once the program began, he strived to keep his eyes locked on the stage. It began right on time with the arrival of the Hawaiian royalty, the *Ali'i* Court. When these had taken their place the dancing began with the *hula kahiko,* the ancient dances that told the stories of old Hawaii.

Soon the guests were treated to a wonderful spectacle as the dancers swayed on a multi-level stage of lush tropical plants and waterfalls, to the beat of the drums oblivious to their surroundings. Their eyes stared into space as if they were in a trance. The lights shining from above gave a surreal atmosphere to the stage. One by one, the various dances were presented to thunderous applause. Almost everyone in the audience was on holiday and Jonathan knew that the music, the sets, and the splendidly attired dancers would have evoked tremendous appreciation even if the quality of the dancing had not been as great as it was.

It was wonderful, but his eyes sought only Oliana and although each dance was a riveting spectacle, he wanted them to be over almost as soon as they had started. He was mesmerized by the *Ote'a*, the archetypal Tahitian dance, with its rapid, insistent drumbeats and quick-moving hip which, although it did not quite tell a story, illustrated themes through hip movements and gestures. He sat enthralled as the Fijians presented the *meke*, a combination of dances with spears and then fans and finally one which was described as the sitting dance—all that to the accompaniment of singing, hand clapping, and the throb of the drums.

With each performance, Jonathan's enjoyment grew and he began to enjoy the program in its entirety, captivated by the similarities and the differences between the islands. And then, suddenly, she was there on stage. When they were introducing themselves to the audience, he could spot her easily enough for she was taller than the other girls. Jonathan watched as Oliana danced delicately as if she was beyond fear, pain and one with the music, the lights and the drums. Tonight she was a performer—nothing else seemed to matter. Tonight she danced as if she had something to say that could not be expressed in any other way but through the dance.

She saw the audience in a blur. A mystical feeling came over her and she was aware only of the beauty that was Hawaii—the surf crashing on the shore, the faraway mountains, the dizzying waterfalls and the majestic and awesome volcanoes. She became one with it all. Nothing else seemed to matter as the drums picked up their cadence and she moved into the rhythm of the dance. The non-natural volcanoes on the stage sprayed a reddish radiance glow on her face giving her an appearance of a mystical melody.

Having written to him about the program, Oliana may have suspected that Jonathan would be in the crowd, but she could not know for certain if he was there. So it was both thrilling and dreamlike for Jonathan to feel as the dance progressed that the simple dignity of her movements seemed to speak to him.

Although her dark eyes were fixed on the ground, he could sense her speaking to him. With a sense of déjà vu, he heard what she was trying to say and could almost feel the anguish in her soul. There must have been at least a dozen dancers in the background but Jonathan had eyes only for his Oliana. He was so caught up that he was oblivious to everyone else around him although there were excited people all around him. She looked like a half-blossom passionate flower to Jonathan. Then as the rhythm picked up, he could see her as possessed. Her spreading arms and other movements became sensitive and before his eyes she was transformed into quite another person, someone he just did not recognize.

That was not the Oliana he knew. In their relationship to date he had seen her very gentle as a woman in love, but never in the role of a powerful woman. It was all a charade, he knew but this was a new facet of her personality. Is it something that she could turn into if she put her mind to it? She looked like she was possessed by spirit and mysticism of volcano goddess, Pele.

By the time he got used to that incarnation of his beloved Oliana, the tempo of the percussion instruments increased and soon they were thumping away in fury. As it seemed to be transformed to the mighty Goddess Pele, angry and wrecking havoc everywhere. He could not believe that the woman in the red and orange skirt with green undersides was his gentle Oliana. Surely this was someone else! This was someone who knew her power and was not afraid to wield it.

Jonathan sat through the performance dumbstruck and then, an hour and a half later, when the drums finally stopped beating and the dancers bowed to the audience he leaped up like almost everyone there and applauded thunderously.

--- 

They sat in the flickering candlelight and talked for a while. There was still a trace of the makeup on her face. After her dance was over Jonathan had gone backstage and had almost dragged her to the huge limo without allowing her to remove the makeup at leisure or to really freshen up. The limo was equipped with all the accessories. Jonathan offered some champagne reminding her of what he had promised a long time ago - to stay together forever as his first vow. They both drank in the same manner as they did a long time ago to remind them of their first time union and their love for each other. In the future though Jonathan knew that he would not be able to afford any of the luxury he used to but in this special and precious moment with Oliana he would do anything to please her and to get her back.

Jonathan moved closer to her and kissed her cheeks and lips over and over again, and then when he drew back and looked at her, Oliana saw the softness in his eyes.

"I'm glad you came, Jonathan," she said softly.

"Me too. I had to see you. I had to know what you were doing here. You know that I love you and that I always will."

Her face lit up as she leaned towards him and then replied quietly, "Yes, I know."

He put his arm around her and said, "I love you more than life."

"I know that, too," she replied.

"But then why did you run away and without a word?"

"I tried telling you many times. But you were preoccupied with your own thoughts. I could not bear your inattentiveness. I wanted to test your love for me. You don't know how happy you made me, Jonathan."

Jonathan did not ask anything more- that was enough. His island flower had blossomed. He was with her - Oliana. "Your performance tonight was wonderful, and to think that you could dance in such a way to bring out the burning fire in me and everyone."

"It makes me feel alive, makes me feel spiritual, too. This is my way of worshiping my Goddess, Pele. I dream about it for hours, I always have. I've been dancing the *hula* since I was a little child. Once I became older, I knew that I was good at it and that I enjoyed it like nothing else. I remember being unable to stop dancing even long after I stopped going to dance classes. I loved the freedom I felt while dancing and the way it made me feel inside. That has evolved into this."

She stopped, gathering her thoughts. Jonathan stared at her wondering what she was going to say next.

"My father and my mother thought I had a special gift and it was she who put me through dance classes."

In the silence that followed Jonathan looked at her lovely face and his heart went out to her. What was he to do with this lovely young woman who had become such a part of his life? The answer came to him almost immediately—Let my Oliana dance as much as she wants. She is happy to be in her homeland, with her people and her culture.

"After having watched you dance tonight, I realize that the dance is your pulse, your heartbeat, your breathing. It's the rhythm of your life and it will always be an expression in time and movement, in happiness, joy, sadness, and even envy."

They started to talk then, hugging and kissing many times, making up for time lost. Afterwards, Oliana tried to remember the last time they had talked like this. They had rarely argued and there was always open discussion, a lot of give and take.

"I need to be closer to my people and my culture. You can understand that, can't you?"

"Yes, I can. But what about us?"

"I need to be with you, now more than ever, Jonathan. How can we question a love that roars through us like a crashing wave or a shooting star? We are meant to be together," she murmured to his ear. Jonathan's heart started to pound deeply. "I'll never let us be apart again. You are part of me. You would always remain the same in my heart from the first day that brought us the love of sunshine, passion of thrusting ocean and heat of firing volcano." Oliana felt emotionally happy and wrapped herself around Jonathan for the rest of the trip.

It did not take long to reach the hotel. Jonathan insisted that he would carry Oliana to the suite. Oliana agreed with a shy and sweet smile.

The flickering candle lights in the suite created a mysterious, out-of-the-world atmosphere – some in light and some in shade. There were heavy scents of plumeria and gardenia all over the place – even the bed was made with the scattered flowers and the flower net was wrapped around the bed. Oliana was overjoyed and speechless to see that Jonathan remembered it vividly and he did not forget their first encounter in Hawaii. Their first love, fresh and new - sharing each other - all came back to her. She wanted it to last eternally.

They stayed in each other's arms for long and precious moments and they did not even notice when it turned into hours. Jonathan's entire world revolved around her - her sweet smile, her love for nature, her spirituality, and mysticism attracted him toward her when he laid eyes on her for the first time and forever.

Kissing her one more time Jonathan said, "You know, Oliana, when you told me life is too short to be unhappy, I did not understand it. You were right. All my life I was never happy. I was always chasing things that I never wanted, only to please others. I had an abundance of money and everything else but that did not make me happy either. I was starving inside for real love. When you left me, it opened my eyes that you are the most important person in my life. You bring me happiness. And in that connection now I also understand why you left me to pursue your dream. I now understand what love means." Oliana did not say a word but felt Jonathan's deep emotions towards her. This simple and pure life in a beautiful tropical land without corruption and with her, Oliana, the love of his life, in this pristine place made Jonathan jubilant and elated. Jonathan continued, "It is so peaceful here. I was so disgusted with life in Houston, always dealing and wheeling, maneuvering everything just to satisfy the greed of my father and others, always self serving. This beautiful tropical land with its blue ocean and the mighty volcanoes bring me peace and something higher and your love made everything possible. Now I can go on with my life and with you being happy."

— — —

# About this book

I always wanted to write a novel which is one-of-a-kind and present a comprehensive and ample idea through a fiction, subject to many interpretations, and heightening perceptions. This book is all of that as it conveys ethical dilemma, corporate corruption, concept of love, importance of romance, present form of spirituality and acceptance of many facets of religions of different cultures of India, America and Hawaii to shape its own spiritualism. Globalization of "God" gave birth to "Spiritualism."

The idea of being wealthy, frugal and socially aware are not new but today I have observed that more and more wealthy young people who are particularly inspired by fairness, spiritualism and love that bring them happiness do not want to be the worshiper of over excessive materials since that takes away their human quality. Often they may even leave the country to get inner peace as they carry the burden of other people's greed, selfishness, and corruption. Instead of their own glory, they embrace modesty as they realize only having overindulgence amount of money and excess amount of material stuff which does not bring real love, happiness or inner peace and in the process they are often tormented by their own ethical conflicts and resolve the conflicts by inducing proper justification for that causes.

Another observation was presented in this novel that now-a-days many people in America and Europe are adopting a secondary faith to shape their own spiritualism. Adopting second faith gave them an opportunity to fulfill the space in their mind where they can establish a direct spiritual connection as well. I have presented this idea through main character like Jonathan, the new generation who has embraced Dalai Lama's Buddhist view with his Christian principle. Jonathan's friend O.C is a product of Indo-American relationship –the gradual adoption of other culture, specifically from India; the Hinduism incorporated into his own culture and shaped its own Christian view. Oliana, the heroine in this book derives her life experience through her deep-rooted ancestral spiritual background and she celebrates with dance, songs and by loving nature to please her goddess in an ancient way even though her primary religion is Christianity.

Most of all, it is a wonderful love story, setting in USA, Hawaii and India. It brings new inspiration and new approach as it has painted the innermost feelings of two people, their first experience of whirl-wind physical romances and then of real love. Their aspirations which will strike a chord as it describes how Jonathan in love with Oliana stands up to the irrational norms set by the society and solves many conflicts to bring happiness to them at the end.

If you like to experience these phenomena that may allure your life and how you can shape your own happiness, love, romance and spirituality through that, then this book will be perfect for you.

# Acknowledgements

I am indebted and grateful to the following colleagues for their advice, assistance and support: Steve Harris, CSG Literary Partners and my friends Christine, Helen and Carol. Thanks to my editor Cynthia Beatty who took time to check grammar and improve the clarity of my manuscript. My heartiest thanks go to my husband.

My special thanks go to Mr. Herb Kawainui Kane who has provided the painting of "Pele, the Volcano Goddess of Hawaii" painted by him as my back and front cover image in my book. He is an artist-historian in Hawaii and his extraordinary artistic career experience has included advertising art, painting, sculpture, publishing art, publishing for National Geographic and postage stamps.

# Dedication

This book is dedicated to my husband, Tapan and my sons, Paul and Jon whom I love very much.